READ BOTTOM UP

DEY ST.

AN IMPRINT OF WILLIAM MORROW PUBLISHERS

READ BOTTOM UP

a novel

BY

NEEL SHAH & SKYE CHATHAM

HarperCollins books may be purchased for educational, business, or sales promotional use. For information please e-mail the Special Markets Department at SPsales@harpercollins.com.

FIRST EDITION

Illustrations by Nina Cosford
Designed by Shannon Plunkett

Library of Congress Cataloging-in-Publication Data has been applied for.

ISBN 978-0-06-226213-4

15 16 17 18 19 OV/RRD 10 9 8 7 6 5 4 3 2 1

This book is dedicated to your best friend,
who saw the whole thing happen.

Authors' Note

We wrote this novel because we were sick of the scenarios: Boy likes girl; girl goes on comically disastrous date with boy. Girl likes boy; boy thinks she hates him, but it turns out this is her way of expressing affection and now they're married. Or girl likes boy; boy doesn't like girl; boy sees a shooting star or a taco and comes to the realization that he has been in love with girl this whole time. We were fine with the novels and the movies and the songs about these stories when we were younger, when we didn't realize how very distant they were from our own romantic realities. But these dating trajectories all have one thing in common: They're neat. Clean. Tidy. And therefore they bear little or no resemblance to our contemporary lives. Because sometimes, when a man and a woman like each other *very* much . . . they make an ill-defined mess.

Tell us if this scenario feels right: A great boy/girl enters your life. You both try to make it work but there's a presence of baggage or a discrepancy of feelings and by month five, you've driven each other crazy and yet, miraculously, you both keep this hope train rolling. The relationship lasts for another three months before slamming into a total communication breakdown and creates disproportionately large wreckage considering this person was *barely* your boyfriend/girlfriend. Sound familiar? It should. After all, you've already written it. It's in your inbox.

Somewhere deep in your Sent Items graveyard are the emails you wrote to your former flame along with the emails you wrote *about* those emails to your best friend. It's all right there—a partial record of your relationship. But what if you could see the whole picture? Not just your side of it. After all, somewhere in the pixelated part of the world is your ex's inbox. Therein lies all sorts of analysis to which you were never privy. What if you could read the whole funny, tragic, wincing train wreck of it all, if you could finally open up your relationship like a dollhouse (or, say, a cadaver) and know the truth of what happened?

Read Bottom Up makes this twisted fantasy a reality. This book is composed entirely of carefully time-stamped emails between our hero (Elliot), our heroine (Madeline), and their respective best friends (David and Emily). But format alone is not what makes this book a mirror of our lives. We also wrote it in real time—emailing from the perspective of two characters apiece—which means that, just as you wouldn't see your boyfriend or girlfriend's emails to his/her best friend, we, as authors, never saw each other's complaints or cries for advice. Nor did we see the well-meaning (but often biased) responses that came back. We're reading half of this book for the first time, same as you. We're seeing the parts of Madeline and Elliot's relationship that we were never meant to see.

And why would we do this to ourselves? Why would we write a half-blind which-way book of the modern heart? Science, friends. Science.

—Neel & Skye

A Visual Key

A conversation between Elliot and Madeline

A conversation between Elliot and David

A conversation between Madeline and Emily

Text Messages

READ BOTTOM UP

MARCH

Salato West
friends & family dinner

JOIN US IN CELEBRATING
THE SOFT (AND OH-SO-CUDDLY)
OPENING OF OUR WESTSIDE OUTPOST.

Sunday, March 2

8PM – 11PM

450 WASHINGTON ST.
NEW YORK CITY

PLEASE RSVP TO SALATOWEST@GMAIL.COM
WE LOOK FORWARD TO SEEING YOU BUT WE'RE
A SMALL SPACE... THIS INVITE ADMITS YOU
AND YOU ONLY.

Subject: Idiot
From: David Meyer <davidmeyer@lathamlaw.com>
Date: Mon, Mar 3 at 9:45 AM
To: Elliot Rowe <elliot@salatowest.com>

You went home with Ellie, didn't you? Please tell me you didn't go home with Ellie.

I know she's way too hot for you and everything, but Jesus, you are a weak, weak man.

Subject: Re: Idiot
From: Elliot Rowe <elliot@salatowest.com>
Date: Mon, Mar 3 at 10:06 AM
To: David Meyer <davidmeyer@lathamlaw.com>

I did not go home with her.

I mean I *did* walk her back to her apartment, tell her I'm still madly in love with her, and offer to stay over (just spoon) and do her laundry in the morning . . . but she said no to everything, so I didn't technically go home with her.

Except the laundry part. She did let me come in and do that.

Subject: Re: Idiot
From: David Meyer <davidmeyer@lathamlaw.com>
Date: Mon, Mar 3 at 10:07 AM
To: Elliot Rowe <elliot@salatowest.com>

The sad thing is I can't actually tell if you're joking or not.

Subject: Re: Idiot
From: Elliot Rowe <elliot@salatowest.com>
Date: Mon, Mar 3 at 11:12 AM
To: David Meyer <davidmeyer@lathamlaw.com>

Dude, relax. I told you, we are just friends ("friends"). We hung out. Made some jokes. I pretended not to eavesdrop when she was talking to that asshole French DJ—who, for the record, I hated before I found out that he's been trying to bang my ex. I saw the card he was giving out to people: "DJ/Model/Freelance Writer." Very curious as to who's ever paid him to write anything.

Subject: Re: Idiot
From: David Meyer <davidmeyer@lathamlaw.com>
Date: Mon, Mar 3 at 12:15 PM
To: Elliot Rowe <elliot@salatowest.com>

I still don't get why you feel the need to have friendly relations with a girl who has basically just existed to make your life miserable for the past year, but you do you, buddy.

BTW—who was that brunette you were talking to when I was leaving? She was cute. That kind of looked like a thing?

And not that I would ever suggest this, because I am not this calculating, but if you REALLY wanted Ellie to like you again, it wouldn't hurt for you to, you know, start dating again.

Hey what should I eat for lunch? I am so sick of everything around my office.

Her name was Madeline. That's kind of a wifey name, right? I feel like I could marry a Madeline.

Guess it's a little weird to associate your future wife with the protagonist of a kids book, but yeah, she was cute. Didn't get her number last night but got her email today.

It's kind of cold out. Ramen? I don't know, stop asking me this every day.

Subject: Is This Awkward?
From: Elliot Rowe <elliot@salatowest.com>
Date: Mon, Mar 3 at 1:12 PM
To: Madeline Whittaker <madeline@fivespoonspress.com>

Hey Madeline,

It's Elliot, the cute scruffy dude who was wearing flannel last night. Wait, that doesn't narrow it down, lemme try again: I was the cute scruffy dude wearing flannel who also worked at the restaurant.

Shit. Still doesn't narrow it down, huh? We talked okay?! For, like, three whole minutes! You told me you loved the brick chicken but that the brussels sprouts were a little overcooked. I said, "Yeah, well why don't you try making perfectly roasted brussels sprouts for 100 drunk people in a restaurant that isn't even technically open yet." (Kidding. I just thought that.) But you left before I got a chance to ask for your number, which is why I had to get it from our PR girl, which is how this email ended up in your inbox.

Anyway. My evenings are a little tied up with said restaurant, but maybe you'd like to get coffee sometime? Like Thursday?

(Here's where you think, "I can't agree to Thursday, that's too soon. Maybe I'll suggest next Tuesday?")

Tuesday works for me too.

—Elliot

--------Forwarded Message-------
Subject: Is This Awkward?
From: Elliot Rowe <elliot@salatowest.com>
Date: Mon, Mar 3 at 1:12 PM
To: Madeline Whittaker <madeline@fivespoonspress.com>

Hey Madeline,

It's Elliot, the cute scruffy dude who was wearing flannel last . . .

Subject: [Fwd: Is This Awkward?]
From: Madeline Whittaker <madeline@fivespoonspress.com>
Date: Mon, Mar 3 at 1:14 PM
To: Emily Roberts <emilyrobertshere@gmail.com>

Presented without comment.
    Okay, presented with *some* comment . . .
    This is the guy I was telling you about. Maybe he doesn't have a girlfriend?

Subject: Re: [Fwd: Is This Awkward?]
From: Emily Roberts <emilyrobertshere@gmail.com>
Date: Mon, Mar 3 at 1:16 PM
To: Madeline Whittaker <madeline@fivespoonspress.com>

He gives good email.
    It's flattering, don't get me wrong, but also maybe a work thing? It almost sounds like a work thing if he's going through the PR person. Plus all the (albeit charming) notes about food.

Subject: Re: [Fwd: Is This Awkward?]
From: Madeline Whittaker <madeline@fivespoonspress.com>
Date: Mon, Mar 3 at 1:20 PM
To: Emily Roberts <emilyrobertshere@gmail.com>

And the coffee. Also: he's a little "tied up" or "tying someone else up," specifically the lightbulb-changing-height blonde he had his arm around half the night. She has a name. Don't ask me what it was since I had difficulty paying attention to this she-beast once I started talking to him . . .

He was cute. First time I've felt that way in a while.

Anyway, charming. Even if it is not a date and he maybe has a girlfriend.

Subject: Re: [Fwd: Is This Awkward?]
From: Emily Roberts <emilyrobertshere@gmail.com>
Date: Mon, Mar 3 at 1:23 PM
To: Madeline Whittaker <madeline@fivespoonspress.com>

Oh, are you the one?

Subject: Re: [Fwd: Is This Awkward?]
From: Madeline Whittaker <madeline@fivespoonspress.com>
Date: Mon, Mar 3 at 1:23 PM
To: Emily Roberts <emilyrobertshere@gmail.com>

The one what?

Subject: Re: [Fwd: Is This Awkward?]
From: Emily Roberts <emilyrobertshere@gmail.com>
Date: Mon, Mar 3 at 1:24 PM
To: Madeline Whittaker <madeline@fivespoonspress.com>

The one who doesn't have access to Facebook?

Subject: Re: [Fwd: Is This Awkward?]
From: Madeline Whittaker <madeline@fivespoonspress.com>
Date: Mon, Mar 3 at 1:31 PM
To: Emily Roberts <emilyrobertshere@gmail.com>

haha. Yes, and I also look for my shoes under the bed. We have like
27 friends in common but i can't see anything but his profile pictures
and they're all of him in glasses/dark alleys behind bars/Coachella
(which is captioned "Brochella" btw. Oy).

Or pictures from when he was a kid. I hate kid pics! It's like, yes,
yes, you were innocent once. Congratulations. Me too.

Maybe you can see more? Plug in "Elliot Rowe" and see.

Subject: Re: [Fwd: Is This Awkward?]
From: Emily Roberts <emilyrobertshere@gmail.com>
Date: Mon, Mar 3 at 1:33 PM
To: Madeline Whittaker <madeline@fivespoonspress.com>

I can't see anything either. But I am rereading this and i think it's a
date. Have you written back yet?

x

Subject: Re: [Fwd: Is This Awkward?]
From: Madeline Whittaker <madeline@fivespoonspress.com>
Date: Mon, Mar 3 at 1:35 PM
To: Emily Roberts <emilyrobertshere@gmail.com>

Nahh, will write tomorrow. Later! xo

Hey Elliot,

   Look at you. I like the detective work, getting my email from Becca. It's just shy of creepy (creepy being "I didn't get your number so I got your address off this W9 you threw away, hope that's cool"). No, kidding, happy you wrote. So glad that things are so busy for you at the restaurant.

   And sure, always happy to break beans (that sounds gross but you get the idea . . .) with a new friend.

   I can't do Thursday but Tuesday works. After work? 6/7ish?

—Madeline

Madeline,

   "Just shy of creepy" is actually my middle name. Seriously, my birth certificate reads, Elliot "Just Shy of Creepy" Rowe. Filling out my name on standardized test forms was always kind of a bummer.

   "New friend," huh? Ouch. At least do me a favor and wait till after the date before putting me in that category. :)
AND YES, I USE EMOTICONS FREQUENTLY AND AM NOT ASHAMED OF IT. AND CAPS LOCK TOO.

   6/7ish, huh? How about 6:18, Broome Street Coffee?

—E"J.S.O.C"R

Subject: Re: Is This Awkward?
From: Madeline Whittaker <madeline@fivespoonspress.com>
Date: Tue, Mar 4 at 12:20 PM
To: Elliot Rowe <elliot@salatowest.com>

Elliot,

Let's say it then. Broome Street works. Though I might show up at 6:19 just to be a big girl about it. I'll be the one with the rose in my teeth. Dangling from the stem will be a slip of paper and on that slip of paper it'll read: "Wait, I thought you had a girlfriend!"

Just kidding. The rose thing has always sounded so painful!

Serious about that last bit though. :)

Looking forward . . .

Madeline

Subject: Re: Is This Awkward?
From: Elliot Rowe <elliot@salatowest.com>
Date: Tue, Mar 4 at 12:42 PM
To: Madeline Whittaker <madeline@fivespoonspress.com>

Wait, the girl I was making awkward small talk with?! That was my *ex*-girlfriend. Jeez, you really think I'd be asking you on a date if 1) I had a girlfriend, and 2) you saw me with her?! I'm not an animal!

And now we've gone and violated the cardinal First Date Rule banning talking about exes. Though I suppose there's nothing in the rule book that says you can't mention them *before* you go out.

See you there.

-------- **Forwarded Message** --------
Subject: Re: Is This Awkward?
From: Elliot Rowe <elliot@salatowest.com>
Date: Tue, Mar 4 at 12:42 PM
To: Madeline Whittaker <madeline@fivespoonspress.com>

Wait, the girl I was making awkward small talk with?! That was my ex-girlfriend. Jeez, do you really think I'd be asking you on a date if . . .

Subject: Re: Is This Awkward?
From: Madeline Whittaker <madeline@fivespoonspress.com>
Date: Tue, Mar 4 at 12:20 PM
To: Elliot Rowe <elliot@salatowest.com>

Elliot,
    Let's say it then. Broome Street works. Though I might show up . . .

Subject: Re: Is This Awkward?
From: Elliot Rowe <elliot@salatowest.com>
Date: Tue, Mar 4 at 12:06 PM
To: Madeline Whittaker <madeline@fivespoonspress.com>

Madeline,
    "Just shy of creepy" is actually my middle name. Seriously . . .

Subject: [Fwd: Re: Is This Awkward?]
From: Madeline Whittaker <madeline@fivespoonspress.com>
Date: Tue, Mar 4 at 12:45 PM
To: Emily Roberts <emilyrobertshere@gmail.com>

Stop the presses! He doesn't have a girlfriend.

Subject: Re: [Fwd: Re: Is This Awkward?]
From: Emily Roberts <emilyrobertshere@gmail.com>
Date: Tue, Mar 4 at 12:47 PM
To: Madeline Whittaker <madeline@fivespoonspress.com>

Oh, this works out VERY nicely because you, i might remind you, don't have a boyfriend. have fun.

Subject: Re: [Fwd: Re: Is This Awkward?]
From: Madeline Whittaker <madeline@fivespoonspress.com>
Date: Tue, Mar 4 at 1:02 PM
To: Emily Roberts <emilyrobertshere@gmail.com>

PS. i am a psycho because i do that thing where whatever greeting/salutation I'm presented with, that's what I reply with. So he left off our names and thus I will too.

Subject: Re: [Fwd: Re: Is This Awkward?]
From: Emily Roberts <emilyrobertshere@gmail.com>
Date: Tue, Mar 4 at 1:13 PM
To: Madeline Whittaker <madeline@fivespoonspress.com>

that's not psychotic, that's called "engaging your mirror." report back.

xo

ONE WEEK LATER...

Elliot

Sorry I kept you out past your bedtime! I promise it won't happen again unless we get your mom to sign a permission slip.

Mar 11, 11:52 PM

Madeline

I forgive you . . . and I had an awesome time too. Not quite awesome enough to put you in touch with my mom yet though.

Mar 12, 12:02 AM

Elliot

Maybe she can just chaperone us next time, middle school dance style? Make sure all hands stay where she can see them?

Mar 12, 10:06 AM

Madeline

You called it. She's like the dad in "Footloose," my mom. Oh and . . . yes to "next time." :)

Mar 12, 10:48 AM

Subject: (no subject)
From: David Meyer <davidmeyer@lathamlaw.com>
Date: Wed, Mar 12 at 10:12 AM
To: Elliot Rowe <elliot@salatowest.com>

How was last night?

Subject: Re: (no subject)
From: Elliot Rowe <elliot@salatowest.com>
Date: Wed, Mar 12 at 11:19 AM
To: David Meyer <davidmeyer@lathamlaw.com>

Was fun. Ended up staying out pretty late and getting kind of drunk.
    She's super funny and cool. I forgot how nice it is hanging out with girls over the age of 25. They're, like, fully-formed humans.

Subject: Re: (no subject)
From: David Meyer <davidmeyer@lathamlaw.com>
Date: Wed, Mar 12 at 1:14 PM
To: Elliot Rowe <elliot@salatowest.com>

You're not allowed to describe girls as "cool" after *Gone Girl*.

You going to see her again?

Subject: Re: (no subject)
From: Elliot Rowe <elliot@salatowest.com>
Date: Wed, Mar 12 at 2:06 PM
To: David Meyer <davidmeyer@lathamlaw.com>

Working nights rest of week and then supposed to see that chick I met at the Bowery Hotel on Friday, so we'll see.

Actually, Bowery girl texted me earlier asking if I had a friend for her friend. Do I have a friend for her friend?

Subject: Re: (no subject)
From: David Meyer <davidmeyer@lathamlaw.com>
Date: Wed, Mar 12 at 2:10 PM
To: Elliot Rowe <elliot@salatowest.com>

You do!

Subject: Re: (no subject)
From: Elliot Rowe <elliot@salatowest.com>
Date: Wed, Mar 12 at 3:01 PM
To: David Meyer <davidmeyer@lathamlaw.com>

Really respect how you said yes to this without even asking for a picture. #hero

---

A FEW DAYS LATER...

Emily

Updates, please.

Mar 17, 10:44 AM

Madeline

I got nothin'. I want to check in but also there's that adage about how if boys want you, they will come after you. You don't have to remind them.

Mar 17, 10:48 AM

Emily

Well, there's also that adage about not buying the cow if you can get the milk for free but WHAT IF YOU'RE LACTOSE INTOLERANT

Mar 17, 10:51 AM

Madeline

Still . . .

Mar 17, 10:56 AM

Emily

Who contacted who last?

Mar 17, 11:00 AM

Madeline

He did. And implied that there wld be a "next time"

Mar 17, 11:07 AM

Emily

Well . . . He already got your email, asked you out, texted you after . . . I don't think you're in any danger of humiliating yourself here

Mar 17, 11:33 AM

Madeline

True. Very true. Okay . . . doing it.

Mar 17, 12:01 PM

Subject: Peep This!
From: Madeline Whittaker <madeline@fivespoonspress.com>
Date: Mon, Mar 17 at 12:04 PM
To: Elliot Rowe <elliot@salatowest.com>

See?: http://www.seriouseats.com/recipes/2010/03/peeps-recipes-how-to-make-peepshi-sushi-rice-krispies-treats-easter.html
   I wouldn't make it up! I mean, I would, but I don't have your culinary genius. Anyway, it was fun to hang out . . . but you knew that. And, sorry I hold my liquor like a college freshman.
   Hope you had a good wknd.

Madeline

Subject: Re: Peep This!
From: Elliot Rowe <elliot@salatowest.com>
Date: Mon, Mar 17 at 1:48 PM
To: Madeline Whittaker <madeline@fivespoonspress.com>

Hey there, freshman!
   My sincere apologies for not getting back to you sooner—restaurant has been insanely busy, which by extension makes me insanely busy. Not that that's an excuse for not reaching out—Tuesday was a lot of fun! (That is not an ironic exclamation point.) We should do it again. Not the exact same thing, mind you—my liver was prepared for "coffee" on Tuesday, not "coffee plus whiskey plus more whiskey plus, oh, what the hell, a little more whiskey." So maybe we get smart and throw food into the mix? Is that crazy? If so, call me crazy! (That is an ironic exclamation point.)
   I have work this wknd, but am free Thursday . . .
   Date number two. I haven't been on a proper second date in more than three years. I better get my game face on.

—EA

Hey there,

In college, we used to have these plastic keg cups for our Spring-fest that said stuff like "Remember: Spring-fest is a marathon, not a sprint!" Which, in retrospect, is a hilarious acquiescing of power on the part of the administration. Like hey, try not to do so many body shots, kids, but if you want to drink from morning until noon like a hobo, we can't stop you. Sorry . . . where was I? Still drunk?

Really, I am just relieved I didn't make an ass out of myself and you want to voluntarily spend more time with me! (Sincere exclamation point.)

Thursday works. What time are you thinking/where?

Also . . . 3 years, huh? I feel like this is a riddle since we now know I've met your ex. So if Elliot broke up with Tall Model six months ago but hasn't asked anyone out for a second date in three years, how long was Elliot dating Tall Model?

—MW

From: Elliot Rowe <elliot@salatowest.com>
Date: Mon, Mar 17 at 4:23 PM
To: Madeline Whittaker <madeline@fivespoonspress.com>

Wellll . . . sometime after whiskey #3 (that, incidentally, is a lyric in every country song ever), you did accidentally fling the contents of your glass at the unsuspecting Asian couple the table over from us.

And then you later admitted that you hadn't had sex since you and your banker boyfriend broke up in January. But those things were more "cute" than you making an ass of yourself. (Also, I'm totally on the hunt for a rebound for you.)

Don't spend too much time on the riddle of the Tall Model. I already made that mistake.

How about dinner? 7ish?

Subject: Re: Peep This!
From: Madeline Whittaker <madeline@fivespoonspress.com>
Date: Mon, Mar 17 at 4:57 PM
To: Elliot Rowe <elliot@salatowest.com>

Oh my god. I forgot about the Asian couple. But since I have never blacked out in my life (really! it's a gift . . . and a curse), I will say that I didn't fling it "at" them—I was reaching out to touch your face and it accidentally slipped from my hand. Apparently whiskey fucks with my depth perception?

Did one of us offer to pay for that lady's dry cleaning? I feel like not and I feel like that's something my mom would want me to do.

Oh, and let's make a deal: I won't bring up the Tall Model and I'm hoping you can let the no-sex-in-months comment slide.

Pun intended.

I look forward to enacting said deal on Thursday at 7. Do you already have somewhere in mind? I can pick.

Totally forgot to offer to pay. We did, however, make some jokes about how they probably own a laundromat, because we are terrible people.

I hereby agree to the terms of your deal. How about Lupa? You can pick the spot after where we hurl shot glasses of tequila at unassuming Mexican couples. You know, switch things up a bit.

Till soon,

Elliot

Elliot

Hey—bummed you had to leave after dinner, you missed a fun show!

Mar 21, 10:28 AM

Madeline

Glad you had fun!

Mar 21, 2:45 PM

. . . it was nice to meet everyone too.

Mar 21, 2:46 PM

Elliot

Probably good you went home when you did. Kinda hurting today . . .

Mar 21, 3:02 PM

Subject: Stop calling my phone
From: Elliot Rowe <elliot@salatowest.com>
Date: Fri, Mar 21 at 11:14 AM
To: David Meyer <davidmeyer@lathamlaw.com>

I don't check my voicemails because I am a human in the 21st century.

Anyway, assume you were calling about Madeline. Had a good time. It was a little weird because we were meeting at Lupa but when I got there, Andy, Will, and Jess and a bunch of people were randomly there, so I sat with them for a drink. And then Madeline showed up and sat with us, and we never actually got our own table? But it was fun. (Jess liked her a lot, and she basically hates every girl I ever date, so that's something.)

Went to some show after, but she dipped out early because she has a normal-person job.

Texted a little with that girl from Tinder after the show, but ended up calling it.

Subject: Re: Stop calling my phone
From: David Meyer <davidmeyer@lathamlaw.com>
Date: Fri, Mar 21 at 12:06 PM
To: Elliot Rowe <elliot@salatowest.com>

I appreciate the detailed play-by-play, but did you and Madeline make out? That's really the only thing I ever want to know.

Subject: Re: Stop calling my phone
From: Elliot Rowe <elliot@salatowest.com>
Date: Fri, Mar 21 at 2:04 PM
To: David Meyer <davidmeyer@lathamlaw.com>

There was a brief kiss goodbye, but I think the briefness was only b/c there were a lot of other people around and she doesn't really strike me as the full-on public make-out type.
  She's a real lady. I could use a lady.

Subject: Re: Stop calling my phone
From: David Meyer <davidmeyer@lathamlaw.com>
Date: Fri, Mar 21 at 2:05 PM
To: Elliot Rowe <elliot@salatowest.com>

Sounds like The One.

Subject: Re: Stop calling my phone
From: Elliot Rowe <elliot@salatowest.com>
Date: Fri, Mar 21 at 2:08 PM
To: David Meyer <davidmeyer@lathamlaw.com>

They're always The One this early. But I do like her. Might even get crazy, call her on the phone this week.

Subject: Re: Stop calling my phone
From: David Meyer <davidmeyer@lathamlaw.com>
Date: Fri, Mar 21 at 3:01 PM
To: Elliot Rowe <elliot@salatowest.com>

Wow. Really going out on a limb.
  Hey, in your professional culinary opinion, what's better: PinkBerry or Yogurtland?

Subject: Re: Stop calling my phone
From: Elliot Rowe <elliot@salatowest.com>
Date: Fri, Mar 21 at 3:06 PM
To: David Meyer <davidmeyer@lathamlaw.com>

PinkBerry all day err day. I don't fuck with that off-brand shit.

Subject: polygamy hits the Northeast
From: Madeline Whittaker <madeline@fivespoonspress.com>
Date: Fri, Mar 21 at 9:45 AM
To: Emily Roberts <emilyrobertshere@gmail.com>

Heya:

Got your text. Sorry, I just shut my phone off and collapsed into bed. No, my exhaustion did not originate with me breaking my dry spell by having sex with Elliot in a coat closet . . . which is kind of impossible these days, actually. Unless you want to have sex in front of the coat check girl or with the coat check girl. Anyway: none was had.

I show up at dinner (i may or may not have gotten a blow-out for this occasion.) Also wore the infamous date shirt that I wore with Rob. Maybe this is a dumb move but I choose not to think of it as "the shirt that started the relationship that nearly killed me" and more as "the shirt that started the relationship . . . ANY relationship."

So I walk into the restaurant and I'm wandering around like a total chump with a cafeteria tray because I can't find Elliot ANYWHERE. So I ask the hostess if a guy came in and she shakes her head. I kind of assume I got the time or the place wrong, which is obviously unlike me, but then, from the end of this big long table, I hear my name.

He was there with a group of about six guys and gals from his restaurant. Or other restaurants. I don't know. All I know is I smiled and sat there and nodded while they all blathered on about how overrated David Chang is for 40 minutes and ooohh whoops, sorry, they had ALREADY ORDERED when I got there. I had to beg a side of fries and drinks off the waiter who had closed out the tab and clearly thought I was the a-hole. Elliot was at the opposite end of the table and I barely spoke to him.

His friends were nice and I talked to some guy about what kinds of pans I should get for my apartment. I had to make instant friends with some chick because i was beyond starving and i thought, well: "We're gonna get real close real fast, lady, because now I have to eat off your plate."

Emily, it was like i was speed dating or at some coworker's birthday that I never signed up for. Everyone asking, "How do you know Elliot?" and then having to explain, to some chef he's known forever, the same answer: "Um . . . he picked me up at a party a couple of weeks ago and now is pawning me off on you?" I'm sure I wasn't very nice since I honestly didn't expect to meet anyone new. But I tried to roll with it. At one point Elliot got up to go to the bathroom and squeezed my shoulders and then SAT BACK DOWN AT THE OTHER END OF THE TABLE. I kept checking my phone thinking there was a "sorry, long story" text waiting for me. Nada.

Then, finally, everyone starts to motivate to leave and Elliot is like, hey, are you coming with us to the show? What? Huh? Whatever: band.

So I said "Sure." Walking over I kind of got stuck talking to a girl and two of his guy friends, laughing at jokes I didn't get about people I had never heard of . . .

Yeah. I lasted about 5 minutes at the show and then it occurred to me, you know what, Madeline? If this isn't even a DATE, there's nothing rude about me faking a work emergency and getting out of here. Not that we're bf/gf, but if Elliot doesn't have to—or even want to :(—make me a priority, I can fake a recipe emergency.

I'm peeved. I don't even know why. I feel like if I was a more chill human I wouldn't even be mad? or would I be?

Madeline x

Subject: Re: polygamy hits the Northeast
From: Emily Roberts <emilyrobertshere@gmail.com>
Date: Fri, Mar 21 at 11:52 AM
To: Madeline Whittaker <madeline@fivespoonspress.com>

Oh. My. Lord. One day (not today, mind you), you'll look back on this and lauuugh and lauuugh.

Sounds like something got sacrificed last night and it wasn't a pig . . . it was Elliot's chances with you. We knew he was a flightypants from day 1 though, right?

Can't believe he hasn't called. Please hold, calling u as soon as I get my students to the lunchroom. x

---

A FEW DAYS LATER...

David

Yooo. What you up to the rest of the week?

Mar 24, 5:06 PM

Elliot

Not a whole lot. Roster's a little depleted.

Mar 24, 5:15 PM

David

Really sorry to hear that. What ever happened to Madeline?

Mar 24, 5:17 PM

Elliot

You know, I don't even really know. I texted her after the show, got the ". . ." bubble from her but then it went away and she didn't write anything, which should basically be illegal. Weird b/c I usually have a good read on whether or not a hang was good and that was def good.

Mar 24, 5:20 PM

David

Hmmm. Maybe call her?

Mar 24, 5:22 PM

Elliot

I'm not a sociopath. I'll try emailing.

Mar 24, 5:26 PM

David

Good call.

Mar 24, 5:27 PM

Subject: Oh, Hello.
From: Elliot Rowe <elliot@salatowest.com>
Date: Tue, Mar 25 at 1:02 PM
To: Madeline Whittaker <madeline@fivespoonspress.com>

Hey Madeline,

Remember me? It's Elliot. We met at a restaurant, went out, made out a couple times. Not that anyone's counting.

Anyway. Not sure if you got my text (well, let's be real: has anyone in human history ever "not" actually gotten the text? As much as I'd like to think that some yet-biologically-unclassified Text Monster came in and ate my message before you read it, I'm pretty sure that's not the case), but in case you didn't, just wanted to say I'd love to hang out again. I thought last week was pretty great, so I guess I'm a little confused by your radio silence?

Obviously, if you didn't have fun/you're no longer into this/you met the man of your dreams and are getting married in Tahiti next weekend, that's cool too.

Actually, if you did meet the man of your dreams, just make up something more palatable. Like, you decided you're into chicks now. Can't argue with that.

—Elliot

---------- Forwarded Message-------
Subject: Oh, Hello.
From: Elliot Rowe <elliot@salatowest.com>
Date: Tue, Mar 25 at 1:02 PM
To: Madeline Whittaker <madeline@fivespoonspress.com>

Hey Madeline,
   Remember me? It's Elliot. We met at a restaurant, went out, made . . .

Subject: [Fwd: Oh, Hello.]
From: Madeline Whittaker <madeline@fivespoonspress.com>
Date: Tue, Mar 25 at 1:06 PM
To: Emily Roberts <emilyrobertshere@gmail.com>

agg. now i feel bad. I mean, yes, i wanted more than a text and this is what i got. but i slightly resent the idea that *I'm* the one who got this awkward train rolling . . .
   But very psyched to hear from him.

Subject: Re: [Fwd: Oh, Hello.]
From: Emily Roberts <emilyrobertshere@gmail.com>
Date: Tue, Mar 25 at 1:14 PM
To: Madeline Whittaker <madeline@fivespoonspress.com>

awww. we like him again. I think you just want men to be smarter than they are, in which case yeah, he has a point: you should date women.

Subject: Re: [Fwd: Oh, Hello.]
From: Madeline Whittaker <madeline@fivespoonspress.com>
Date: Tue, Mar 25 at 1:30 PM
To: Emily Roberts <emilyrobertshere@gmail.com>

Ha. I tried that for a day in college. But yeah . . . okay, i think i need to be more chill and less stringent and expand my horizons. Maybe i can start by not actively waiting for guys to disappoint me . . .

Subject: Re: [Fwd: Oh, Hello.]
From: Emily Roberts <emilyrobertshere@gmail.com>
Date: Tue, Mar 25 at 2:40 PM
To: Madeline Whittaker <madeline@fivespoonspress.com>

well, it's good that you recognize this habit. I read his e-mail and think: he's like a puppy you locked in the bathroom for peeing on the floor and he clearly has NO IDEA what he did or didn't do. And now he's whimpering to be let out.

   In the words of the Baha Men*: Let the dogs out. Be the one to let the dogs out.

xo Em

*(Yes, i had to Wikipedia this.)

Subject: Re: Oh, Hello.
From: Madeline Whittaker <madeline@fivespoonspress.com>
Date: Tue, Mar 25 at 4:09 PM
To: Elliot Rowe <elliot@salatowest.com>

Sorry, who is this? So many Elliots, it's hard to keep track.

Too soon? I did, in fact, get your text. Sorry about the belated reply.

Honestly, I had a great time the other night and I really enjoyed meeting your friends (Jess especially), but I was a little bit taken aback when I ran out of work early, showed up at the restaurant looking for one human and found a small tribe of them. It's honestly not a huge deal but at some point your friend Jess was like "Are you coming with us to the show?" and in my brain I was all, "Well all of you guys came on my date so I guess so". . . . Anyway, sorry to kiss and run Cinderella-style, but I had a 9 AM marketing meeting I couldn't miss. Hope it's not weird that I'm typing all this and so early on. It's not indicative of me being "no longer into this." What you see in the previous—wait, let me count—five lines is exactly how much it irked me.

I would love to hang out soon with a little less Group Date ("The Bachelor") and a little more One on One ("The Bachelor").

—mw

--------Forwarded Message-------
Subject: Re: Oh, Hello.
From: Madeline Whittaker <madeline@fivespoonspress.com>
Date: Tue, Mar 25 at 4:09 PM
To: Elliot Rowe <elliot@salatowest.com>

Sorry, who is this? So many Elliots, it's hard to keep track.
  Too soon? I did, in fact, get your text. Sorry about the belated . . .

Subject: [Fwd: Re: Oh, Hello.]
From: Elliot Rowe <elliot@salatowest.com>
Date: Tue, Mar 25 at 5:22 PM
To: David Meyer <davidmeyer@lathamlaw.com>

Well, look who's back. And evidently mad at me.

Subject: Re: [Fwd: Re: Oh, Hello.]
From: David Meyer <davidmeyer@lathamlaw.com>
Date: Tue, Mar 25 at 5:48 PM
To: Elliot Rowe <elliot@salatowest.com

"What you see in the previous—wait, let me count—five lines is exactly how much it irked me."
  She's not mad. She's irked! (Kind of justifiably, too.)
  I mean, you have been saying that you're looking for someone who is gonna call you on your shit . . . though there's a huge difference between what you "say" you're looking for and what you "are" looking for.
  Basically I could see you guys either getting married or hating each other in 6 months. Kind of a toss-up!

-------Forwarded Message-------
Subject: Re: Oh, Hello.
From: Madeline Whittaker <madeline@fivespoonspress.com>
Date: Tue, Mar 25 at 4:09 PM
To: Elliot Rowe <elliot@salatowest.com>

Sorry, who is this? So many Elliots, it's hard to keep track.
    Too soon? I did, in fact, get your text. Sorry about the belated . . .

Subject: me = asshole?
From: Madeline Whittaker <madeline@fivespoonspress.com>
Date: Tue, Mar 25 at 9:42 PM
To: Emily Roberts <emilyrobertshere@gmail.com>

Oh crap. I haven't heard back from him yet. Was this bad? Did I just
back him into an "us" talk?

Subject: Re: me = asshole?
From: Emily Roberts <emilyrobertshere@gmail.com>
Date: Tue, Mar 25 at 10:15 PM
To: Madeline Whittaker <madeline@fivespoonspress.com>

Listen, if this is what scares him away, he was meant to be scared.
I think it's good that you were honest with him but I think it would
have been even better if you were honest *at the time*. Not because
honesty is so great but because it would have just taken up less
emotional space than this. You could have just pulled him aside
when you were walking to the show and been like, "Looks like we
have company, huh?"
    Because like I said: puppy didn't know what he was doing . . .
Bedtime. xo Em

Subject: Re: Oh, Hello.
From: Elliot Rowe <elliot@salatowest.com>
Date: Tue, Mar 25 at 11:00 PM
To: Madeline Whittaker <madeline@fivespoonspress.com>

There you are! I was worried sick!

Well, I'm glad the reason for your belated response wasn't a Text Monster, but me being an idiot.

Totally my bad on the group dinner front—definitely didn't mean for you to read into it. For the record, those guys all really liked you. Especially Jess. And she literally hates everyone. I'm still not even sure she likes me.

Anyway, again. Sorry. And yes—a "Bachelor"-style one-on-one date would be great. Might be hard to rent a helicopter that'll take us to a remote Swiss chalet on such short notice, but I can take you to a movie . . .

Chris Harrison will be conducting a postmortem, though.

APRIL

Elliot

Psyched for our DATE (all caps) tonight. Look, I even picked up a rose: ----{@

Apr 1, 4:12 PM

Madeline

You're not eligible to get a rose until AFTER we go out. Respect the rules of the game!

Apr 1, 4:25 PM

Elliot

Well, if we're playing by the rules, I call you Madeline W and you call me Elliot R. The world only finds out our real names when we're WINNERS.

Apr 1, 4:30 PM

Madeline

By "winners," do you mean we make an ill-conceived decision to get married on national television and then break up six months later?

Apr 1, 4:31 PM

Elliot

Exactly. You can have the sympathetic "Us Weekly" cover but I call dibs on the "Dancing with the Stars" appearance.

Apr 1, 4:32 PM

Madeline

Deal. See you at the theater at 8! Really looking forward to "putting myself out there" and "believing in this process."

Apr 1, 4:33 PM

Elliot

BUT ARE YOU IN IT FOR THE RIGHT REASONS??

Apr 1, 4:34 PM

Madeline

ALWAYS

Apr 1, 4:34 PM

Subject: (no subject)
From: Elliot Rowe <elliot@salatowest.com>
Date: Wed, Apr 2 at 10:52 AM
To: Madeline Whittaker <madeline@fivespoonspress.com>

So, uh, sorry again about the Great Movie Fiasco of '14. Next time I invite you to see "Annie Hall" at the Angelika, I promise I'll buy tickets beforehand. (I still can't believe it was sold out. I kind of figured everyone in New York had seen it by now) . . . I will say, though, that yesterday's walk-out of consolation prize "Big Daddy 2: Bigger Daddy" marks the fourth time I've ever bailed on a movie I've paid money to see, "Encino Man," "Nutty Professor II: The Klumps," and "Love and Other Drugs" being the other three. And to walk out of a movie where Anne Hathaway's naked the whole time, well, that says something . . .

Subject: Re: (no subject)
From: Madeline Whittaker <madeline@fivespoonspress.com>
Date: Wed, Apr 2 at 11:46 AM
To: Elliot Rowe <elliot@salatowest.com>

You walked out of "Encino Man"? What were you, 12? Where did you go? Actually, don't answer that. I like the image of you furiously riding away from the theater on your bike, grinding your teeth against your retainer. It's kind of cute. Tell me . . . do you still possess said retainer?

Subject: Re: (no subject)
From: Elliot Rowe <elliot@salatowest.com>
Date: Wed, Apr 2 at 5:45 PM
To: Madeline Whittaker <madeline@fivespoonspress.com>

Sorry—phone died when I was out. You know how it goes. Why do iPhones suddenly go from 11% battery to dead? What happened to that 11%? These are the things that keep me up at night.

Anyway, what are you doing tomorrow? I'm off and I was planning on spending it getting stoned and seeing if "Encino Man" is as bad as I remember. Care to join? Lemme know and I'll see if I can find the retainer.

Subject: Re: (no subject)
From: Madeline Whittaker <madeline@fivespoonspress.com>
Date: Wed, Apr 2 at 7:48 PM
To: Elliot Rowe <elliot@salatowest.com>

I do know how it goes. My friend Emily dropped her phone in a public toilet once. I was brought in as a witness when the guy she was seeing didn't believe THAT was the reason for her lack of communication.

Yeah, that sounds cool! Just don't get handsy. I mean: do? I mean: you find your retainer and if you're VERY lucky I'll find my sexy Snow White costume. I drowned in that thing when I was 15. I'm sure I'd look like a milkmaid in it now . . .

I can't do during the day (obviously), but let me know what time.

M

David

What you doing tonight? There's a party on Ludlow for this "artisanal" vodka company we do work for that I might swing by.

Apr 3, 6:06 PM

Elliot

Staying in. Madeline's coming over.

Apr 3, 6:14 PM

David

But the vodka is made by artisans!

Apr 3, 6:16 PM

Also, twice in three days? Look at you.

Apr 3, 6:16 PM

Elliot

The heart wants what the heart wants, David ;)

Apr 3, 6:20 PM

David

You really have to stop using emoticons.

Apr 3, 6:21 PM

Madeline

It's 8:45 AM and I am eating a bagel and lox from Russ and Daughters.

Apr 4, 8:45 AM

Emily

Fascinating.

Apr 4, 8:57 AM

Madeline

THINK.

Apr 4, 8:58 AM

Emily

. . . Oh! Because you don't live near there and Elliot does. You sloot!

Apr 4, 8:59 AM

Madeline

We so totally did it. And maybe everyone on the Bowery saw us because he doesn't have blinds?

Apr 4, 9:06 AM

Emily

Classy. How was it?

Apr 4, 9:07 AM

Madeline

How do you think? :)

Apr 4, 9:07 AM

Subject: Re: (no subject)
From: Elliot Rowe <elliot@salatowest.com>
Date: Fri, Apr 4 at 11:42 AM
To: Madeline Whittaker <madeline@fivespoonspress.com>

Last night again soon, please.

Also: you are very adorable when you're stoned. And also clearly something of a genetic freak. Seriously, I have no idea how someone who finished that entire plate of spaghetti bolognese could also be the same person who looks like *that*.

Subject: Re: (no subject)
From: Madeline Whittaker <madeline@fivespoonspress.com>
Date: Fri, Apr 4 at 12:02 PM
To: Elliot Rowe <elliot@salatowest.com>

Oh my god, I seriously never smoke. I think it would make my job a nightmare. I mean, not that I would smoke at work, but more that I work in dangerously close proximity to a test kitchen . . . and we just finished shooting a gluten-free cookbook. I have never seen so many brownies and blondies (in racial harmony) in one spot.

　　Also, you're the best for saying that I'm a genetic freak. I'm not, but it helps to . . . work out? . . . after. :)

x

TWO WEEKS LATER...

Elliot

Didn't go to the gym today. Any chance my personal trainer is available for another session??

Apr 18, 8:45 PM

Madeline

I will have to consult with her but I'm pretty sure she can squeeze you in . . .

Apr 18, 8:47 PM

Elliot

Gonna have to buy sessions in bulk!

Apr 18, 9:02 PM

Madeline

side note: i am so happy that was your response because the second I sent that I was all: "am i making myself sound like an overscheduled prostitute?"

Apr 18, 9:06 PM

Elliot

Be over like 10ish :)

Apr 18, 9:11 PM

Madeline

This gym keeps really weird hours.

Apr 18, 9:13 PM

David

Yoo what's up.

Apr 24, 7:15 PM

Cool.

Apr 24, 9:05 PM

Remember when we used to hang out?

Apr 24, 9:42 PM

Me neither.

Apr 24, 10:05 PM

I love talking to myself.

Apr 24, 10:42 PM

Elliot

lol sorry. Buddy! I miss you! Dinner this week?

Apr 25, 8:32 AM

David

The young prince emerges from his lair! I'd like that. Just let me know when works for his majesty.

Apr 25, 8:54 AM

Elliot

Hey do you have blinds in your bedroom?

Apr 25, 6:14 PM

David

Yes. I'm an adult. Why?

Apr 25, 9:45 PM

Subject: So . . .
From: Elliot Rowe <elliot@salatowest.com>
Date: Sat, Apr 26 at 11:48 AM
To: Madeline Whittaker <madeline@fivespoonspress.com>

You'll never guess where I am right now . . .

Subject: Re: So . . .
From: Madeline Whittaker <madeline@fivespoonspress.com>
Date: Sat, Apr 26 at 12:14 PM
To: Elliot Rowe <elliot@salatowest.com>

You . . . are . . . in a nutshell? At the restaurant? Standing creepily outside my window even though that's impossible because my apartment doesn't face the street?

Subject: Re: So . . .
From: Elliot Rowe <elliot@salatowest.com>
Date: Sat, Apr 26 at 12:36 PM
To: Madeline Whittaker <madeline@fivespoonspress.com>

I am . . .
   (drum roll, please . . .)
   At Bed, Bath and Beyond. Buying curtains. For my bedroom. No biggie.
   Do I get "mocha," "pearl," or "off-white"?? Tie-back or hook? Do I need "Thermaliner panels"? What are "Thermaliner panels"?! I think I am losing my mind.
   This very nice saleslady is also trying to convince me that I need to buy "window treatments" to really "complete the look." Which, on the box, look to me just like "curtains," but which are evidently a

separate, much more expensive thing? Pretty sure she just works off commission and smells blood in the water. MORE AS THIS STORY DEVELOPS.

Subject: Re: So . . .
From: Elliot Rowe <elliot@salatowest.com>
Date: Sat, Apr 26 at 12:40 PM
To: Madeline Whittaker <madeline@fivespoonspress.com>

Oh my god, now this woman is trying to foist "blackout window curtain liners" on me.

Me: What do those do?
Her: They're great, they really keep the light out.
Me: (confused) I don't understand. Isn't that the function of curtains? To keep out the light?
Her: Yeah, but they're better than curtains.

THEN WHY DO I EVEN NEED THE CURTAINS, LADY? WHAT IS THIS HOME-FURNISHING PONZI SCHEME?
(Obviously I bought them because I am a sucker. Now a fun game will be to see how long this stuff sits in a box in my apartment before I actually set it up.)

Subject: Re: So . . .
From: Madeline Whittaker <madeline@fivespoonspress.com>
Date: Sat, Apr 26 at 1:45 PM
To: Elliot Rowe <elliot@salatowest.com>

I am amazed. Is this my influence? Careful with that place, I go in for a shower curtain liner and come out with, like, a Vagina Swiffer (TM).
Those panels are for people who live in Arizona and need to keep the light out during the day and then need it not to be freezing at night. Ignore them, they're a rip-off. I don't think the Bed, Bath and Beyond people work on commission. How sad. I just think the saleslady doesn't know that your "look" consists of a sofa and a bunch of random vinyl lined up next to a radiator.
In summation: you want "semi-sheer" and a little longer than you think you'll need.

Anyway. Off to copyedit flour measurements. What did people in my job do before they could google embarrassing things like "how many cups in a quart"?

Your walking consumer reports,
M x

PS. They won't sit in a box . . . I'll help you if you want!

Subject: Yo
From: David Meyer <davidmeyer@lathamlaw.com>
Date: Mon, Apr 28 at 11:34 AM
To: Elliot Rowe <elliot@salatowest.com>

So I just checked and that Hudson Valley house is still available this weekend. That work? Let me know and I'll put the deposit down and you can pay me back sometime in the next six to eight months.

Subject: Re: Yo
From: Elliot Rowe <elliot@salatowest.com>
Date: Mon, Apr 28 at 1:06 PM
To: David Meyer <davidmeyer@lathamlaw.com>

Sounds good. Lemme know how much I owe (and I will Paypal you immediately, dick).

Subject: Re: Yo
From: David Meyer <davidmeyer@lathamlaw.com>
Date: Mon, Apr 28 at 2:14 PM
To: Elliot Rowe <elliot@salatowest.com>

That'll depend on total headcount. Is your gf coming?

Subject: Re: Yo
From: Elliot Rowe <elliot@salatowest.com>
Date: Mon, Apr 28 at 2:45 PM
To: David Meyer <davidmeyer@lathamlaw.com>

Wouldn't exactly say she's my girlfriend just yet, but I'll ask.

Subject: Re: Yo
From: David Meyer <davidmeyer@lathamlaw.com>
Date: Mon, Apr 28 at 3:15 PM
To: Elliot Rowe <elliot@salatowest.com>

What do you mean she's not your girlfriend?
　You hang out multiple times a week, neglect your friends, and aren't sleeping with anyone else. (Well I'm assuming she's not.) That pretty much reads "relationship" to me.

Subject: Re: Yo
From: Elliot Rowe <elliot@salatowest.com>
Date: Mon, Apr 28 at 4:56 PM
To: David Meyer <davidmeyer@lathamlaw.com>

I don't know, still feels early. We both have our own shit going on, and it doesn't seem like she's in a rush to just jump into something.

Subject: Re: Yo
From: David Meyer <davidmeyer@lathamlaw.com>
Date: Mon, Apr 28 at 5:02 PM
To: Elliot Rowe <elliot@salatowest.com>

Yeah, you're right. I'm sure she's totally cool with you guys sleeping together all the time and being invited on a weekend getaway with all your friends and she has no expectations about anything whatsoever. Because that's how girls are.

Subject: Re: Yo
From: Elliot Rowe <elliot@salatowest.com>
Date: Mon, Apr 28 at 5:20 PM
To: David Meyer <davidmeyer@lathamlaw.com>

So you're saying I shouldn't bring her?

Subject: Re: Yo
From: David Meyer <davidmeyer@lathamlaw.com>
Date: Mon, Apr 28 at 5:50 PM
To: Elliot Rowe <elliot@salatowest.com>

You're an idiot.

Subject: Re: Yo
From: Elliot Rowe <elliot@salatowest.com>
Date: Mon, Apr 28 at 7:45 PM
To: David Meyer <davidmeyer@lathamlaw.com>

You're mean.

Subject: Heyo!
From: Elliot Rowe <elliot@salatowest.com>
Date: Tue, Apr 29 at 6:00 PM
To: Madeline Whittaker <madeline@fivespoonspress.com>

Sooo . . .

So here's the link to the house (barn?) I was talking about. Looks pretty awesome.

http://www.vrbo.com/31189#photos

I think David (who you met) and Eric are going up Thursday. Everyone else is leaving Fri. afternoon. If you can get out of work a little early, we could probably hitch a ride? If not, happy to Zip Car it.

I think you've probably met most of the people there, other than whatever random chicks David and Eric wrangle this week. I can't imagine we'll do anything more strenuous than go apple picking or sit in a hot tub and drink bourbon, but I'm not really mad at those things, so I'm okay with it.

(Oh. Looks like there are only two actual bedrooms, but given the fact that I'll probably end up doing most of the cooking, I think I'll be able to call dibs on one . . .)

This looks great. Is it weird to ask for a Zip Car in this scenario? I could probably get out of work early but I feel like I've been staying out pretty late and showing up kind of half-mast. So probably can't realistically leave until 4, which would put us on a highway at 4:45 at the earliest. Or we can take the train. I looked up schedules and it looks like they run at hour intervals between Grand Central and the sticks. So we would be catching the 5:07. Assuming someone from your crew can pick us up . . .

Anyway . . . I'm psyched. Let me know about the logistics.

xo

_____

Madeline

I have a sex hangover.

Apr 30, 8:37 AM

Emily

What is wrong with you.

Apr 30, 8:39 AM

Also: I am happy one of us is having any/great sex. That good, huh?

Apr 30, 8:39 AM

Madeline

Kind of amazing? And it's never kind of amazing for me, not in the very beginning. Headed upstate with him and a bunch of ppl this weekend.

Apr 30, 8:42 AM

Emily

!!!!!!!!

Apr 30, 8:42 AM

Madeline

You want to get in on the house?

Apr 30, 9:23 AM

Appreciated but . . . I don't need to detail the 100 ways that sounds like a horror show for me, right? :) Have fun, though. Have lots of s-e-x for me.

Apr 30, 9:44 AM

Madeline

Ha. Isn't that like telling people who go to the beach to "get tan for you?"

Apr 30, 9:45 AM

Emily

Just be a doll and try. xo

Apr 30, 10:06 AM

MAY

Subject: (no subject)
From: Madeline Whittaker <madeline@fivespoonspress.com>
Date: Mon, May 5 at 8:54 AM
To: Elliot Rowe <elliot@salatowest.com>

Soo . . . I am currently in a massive meeting with some Food Network chef who is throwing a hissy fit over the layout of his book (he thinks there are "too many pictures of his hands and not enough of his face"). To distract myself, I am going to make a list of my favorite things from this weekend, in order:

1) Watching David and Eric convince The Girls (still not sure I can tell them apart) to play spin the bottle.
2) Watching David's and Eric's faces when David got Eric three times in a row.
3) Watching David and Eric awkwardly kiss three times.

Oh yeah. You (and your turkey chili) were pretty great too.

Banner weekend, chef. ·

Maddy x

A FEW DAYS LATER...

Subject: (no subject)
From: Elliot Rowe <elliot@salatowest.com>
Date: Fri, May 9 at 11:43 AM
To: Madeline Whittaker <madeline@fivespoonspress.com>

I was thinking you really need to get a coffeemaker. Seriously, how do you not own one?!

Subject: Re: (no subject)
From: Madeline Whittaker <madeline@fivespoonspress.com>
Date: Fri, May 9 at 12:09 PM
To: Elliot Rowe <elliot@salatowest.com>

Because we have coffee at the office and I don't have many overnight guests?

Subject: Re: (no subject)
From: Elliot Rowe <elliot@salatowest.com>
Date: Fri, May 9 at 12:34 PM
To: Madeline Whittaker <madeline@fivespoonspress.com>

I've never worked in an office. What's it like? Tell me everything!

Subject: Re: (no subject)
From: Madeline Whittaker <madeline@fivespoonspress.com>
Date: Fri, May 9 at 12:45 PM
To: Elliot Rowe <elliot@salatowest.com>

Omg amazing. It's like you were hatched out of a free-will womb!
   In an office they not only keep you in ass-fattening identical chairs, sitting under fluorescent lights, but they force you to drink coffee from freeze-dried packets and it's so weak, I'd make tea out of the water that comes out. Save me. :(

Subject: Re: (no subject)
From: Elliot Rowe <elliot@salatowest.com>
Date: Fri, May 9 at 1:30 PM
To: Madeline Whittaker <madeline@fivespoonspress.com>

I just ate a quarter pound of Iberico ham out of our fridge.

Subject: Re: (no subject)
From: Madeline Whittaker <madeline@fivespoonspress.com>
Date: Fri, May 9 at 1:56 PM
To: Elliot Rowe <elliot@salatowest.com>

That's the most sexual thing I've ever heard.

I'll be free by 7:30 btw.

Subject: Re: (no subject)
From: Elliot Rowe <elliot@salatowest.com>
Date: Fri, May 9 at 3:12 PM
To: Madeline Whittaker <madeline@fivespoonspress.com>

Wait, did I black out and forget we have plans tonight? I'm supposed to get drinks with Eric and Jess . . .

Subject: Re: (no subject)
From: Madeline Whittaker <madeline@fivespoonspress.com>
Date: Fri, May 9 at 3:55 PM
To: Elliot Rowe <elliot@salatowest.com>

Oh, no . . . honestly, I just kind of assumed we were hanging out.
I don't know why. Sorry to be unclear. I was saying that I *am* free
starting around 7:30. Been a total zombie (long week). x.

Subject: Re: (no subject)
From: Elliot Rowe <elliot@salatowest.com>
Date: Fri, May 9 at 4:15 PM
To: Madeline Whittaker <madeline@fivespoonspress.com>

Why don't you just text me when you're off work and I'll let you know
what we're doing?

Subject: Re: (no subject)
From: Madeline Whittaker <madeline@fivespoonspress.com>
Date: Fri, May 9 at 4:26 PM
To: Elliot Rowe <elliot@salatowest.com>

Great. Sounds like a plan.

Madeline

Hey, just got out of work, running home to change/etc. Still out/near?

May 9, 7:42 PM

Elliot

Hey! So slight change of plan—we decided to go to this gallery opening in Bushwick. Figured since you're already tired, why don't you just get some zzz and I'll catch up with you this wknd? Brunch maybe?

May 9, 8:06 PM

Madeline

Sorry, was in the subway. All good. Have fun. I have a ton of stuff to do this weekend though. Can we make brunch early?

May 9, 9:12 PM

---------Forwarded Message----------
Subject: Re: (no subject)
From: Madeline Whittaker <madeline@fivespoonspress.com>
Date: Fri, May 9 at 3:55 PM
To: Elliot Rowe <elliot@salatowest.com>

Oh, no . . . honestly, I just kind of assumed we were hanging out. I
don't know why. Sorry to be unclear. I was saying that I *am* free . . .

Subject: Re: (no subject)
From: Elliot Rowe <elliot@salatowest.com>
Date: Fri, May 9 at 3:12 PM
To: Madeline Whittaker <madeline@fivespoonspress.com>

Wait, did I black out and forget we have plans tonight? I'm
supposed to get drinks with Eric and Jess . . .

Subject: [Fwd: Re: (no subject)]
From: Madeline Whittaker <madeline@fivespoonspress.com>
Date: Fri, May 9 at 10:15 PM
To: Emily Roberts <emilyrobertshere@gmail.com>

Read bottom up. So this is what is going on. I don't know. Am I nuts?
I feel this kind of tacit step back on his part?

In a way I am obsessing about this on purpose. Because I know
that "be yourself" is the name of the game, especially at this stage
when we should be past games. So I have this theory that I can get
to a state of "casual" by exhausting myself with analysis. Like a cat
chasing its own tail.

Anyway, I kind of want to just ask him what's up but then I feel
like it will turn into a "talk" that gets clocked in the context of the
relationship and kind of chips away at that blissful beginning time.
I'm not saying I am going to marry Elliot (though I would have

amazing dinners for the rest of my life) but let's just say we did, let's say we're old people in rocking chairs (go with it) and we're looking back over our lives being like, "Grandkids, when we were first together it was so romantic! But then Grandpa avoided defining us, kept weird hours, backtracked, flaked, and Grandma freaked the fuck out and didn't know where she stood. . . . Now, someone get me my bunion cream."

Anyway, I was (am?) so excited because guess what? I finagled an opportunity for us to check into the Four Seasons for the night (next wk). Staying in hotels in one's own city! Hot! Romantic! And screw the weird vibes, I'm still going to ask him (and force him to make actual plans – oh, the horror). One tiny lie? I kind of talked my author (who the suite was actually meant for) into staying with friends because she's a Norwegian chef who I convinced would be lonely in a big fancy hotel . . . I am the devil. And could get into real trouble with this, especially since promotion budgets aren't what they used to be. This guy is driving me to a life of crime?

Love and straitjackets,
Mad

----------Forwarded Message----------
Subject: Re: (no subject)
From: Madeline Whittaker <madeline@fivespoonspress.com>
Date: Fri, May 9 at 3:55 PM
To: Elliot Rowe <elliot@salatowest.com>

Oh, no . . . honestly, I just kind of assumed we were hanging out. I don't know why. Sorry to be unclear. I was saying that I *am* free . . .

Subject: Re: (no subject)
From: Elliot Rowe <elliot@salatowest.com>
Date: Fri, May 9 at 3:12 PM
To: Madeline Whittaker <madeline@fivespoonspress.com>

Wait, did I black out and forget we have plans tonight? I'm supposed to get drinks with Eric and Jess . . .

Subject: [Fwd: Re: (no subject)]
From: Elliot Rowe <elliot@salatowest.com>
Date: Fri, May 9 at 11:17 PM
To: David Meyer <davidmeyer@lathamlaw.com>

So I think you were right

Subject: Re: [Fwd: Re: (no subject)]
From: David Meyer <davidmeyer@lathamlaw.com>
Date: Fri, May 9 at 11:30 PM
To: Elliot Rowe <elliot@salatowest.com>

I'm right about most things. You're going to have to be more specific.

Subject: Re: [Fwd: Re: (no subject)]
From: Elliot Rowe <elliot@salatowest.com>
Date: Fri, May 9 at 11:33 PM
To: David Meyer <davidmeyer@lathamlaw.com>

About me needing to clarify things with Madeline.

  Seeing her tomorrow for brunch, though not exactly sure what I'm gonna say.

Subject: Re: [Fwd: Re: (no subject)]
From: David Meyer <davidmeyer@lathamlaw.com>
Date: Fri, May 9 at 11:54 PM
To: Elliot Rowe <elliot@salatowest.com>

Obviously do what you want, you're a grown up, etc., but I will say one thing: Do you even remember how much of a struggle it was getting Ellie to date you in the first place? I do, because you bitched about it constantly. First she wanted to hang out, then she pulled back, then she'd text you obsessively for a week, then you wouldn't hear from her for a few days, then she'd say come over right now, then she'd make you leave, then she'd say "No, wait, turn the cab around come back." She basically gave you full-blown Stockholm Syndrome. But you got so addicted to the drama you stuck it out way longer than you should have.

  Madeline, on the other hand, has been cool and accommodating and seems well-adjusted and seems to like you, which you now don't even know how to process, because you're so conditioned to only like girls who treat you like shit.

  So, yeah, do what you want, but I thought you should at least be aware of that before you do something dumb.

Subject: Re: [Fwd: Re: (no subject)]
From: Elliot Rowe <elliot@salatowest.com>
Date: Fri, May 9 at 11:58 PM
To: David Meyer <davidmeyer@lathamlaw.com>

There's a reason you're a lawyer and I make kale salad for a living.

THE NEXT DAY...

Elliot

So I guess I have a girlfriend

May 10, 1:15 PM

David

The best part of this text is I can't tell if that means the talk was good or bad. Either way, congrats!

May 10, 1:17 PM

Subject: (no subject)
From: Elliot Rowe <elliot@salatowest.com>
Date: Sun, May 11 at 11:54 AM
To: Madeline Whittaker <madeline@fivespoonspress.com>

Hey,

Just wanted to say that I'm really glad we talked. Believe it or not, while I have many talents, being able to immediately tell what's bothering you isn't one (yet).

Going forward, I am going to try to be as open/direct as possible. Hopefully, that will save us a lot of time and energy that can be better spent on other things. Like making out.

Obviously, we're still kind of figuring this thing out, but that seems like something we can both agree on. Deal?

"Sounds good, Elliot! By the way, you're super handsome. Just thought you should know!"

(Felt like I was on a roll, so just took the liberty of responding for you.) :)

Sincerely, Boyfriend(!)

Subject: Re: (no subject)
From: Madeline Whittaker <madeline@fivespoonspress.com>
Date: Sun, May 11 at 12:36 PM
To: Elliot Rowe <elliot@salatowest.com>

Hey back,

I am happy we talked too. And you are handsome!

I think the thing is (how come there only ever gets to be one "thing" in these conversations?) that we obviously really like each other (hopefully this is obvious . . . sign me up for sex/snuggling/so forth please) but sometimes it's hard to know the degree of on-board-ness the other person is experiencing. And so I don't always feel comfortable saying when something bothers me because it either feels naggy or like I haven't earned the right to say it because I'm not sure where we stand/I stand with you. Just, further to our chat—which was relatively painless, considering!—I want to be honest. I guess what I'm saying is that I'm a firm believer in the proportionate response. And we're still figuring out what this is, so proportions are tricky. Anyway, you're awesome.

And, this email is waaaay too us-talk-y. The cooler reply goes something like:

"It's all good, Elliot. Now, call in sick to work because one of my big authors has just decided to stay with friends when she comes to New York on her book tour and I have not yet canceled her sweet SUITE at the Four Seasons *this week* . . ."

DO IT. Call me when you get this.

Girlfriend(!)

Subject: Re: (no subject)
From: Elliot Rowe <elliot@salatowest.com>
Date: Sun, May 11 at 8:06 PM
To: Madeline Whittaker <madeline@fivespoonspress.com>

Just seeing this because the kitchen is a madhouse right now as two of our line cooks went home early because of food poisoning (irony! and no, not from eating here) but—BUT—I wanted to let you know that I'm glad we're on the same page. Call soon.

P.S. Agreed. People who are dating and live in the same city shouldn't have to write emails that are this long to each other. So let's try not to do it anymore. :)

Subject: (no subject)
From: Emily Roberts <emilyrobertshere@gmail.com>
Date: Mon, May 12 at 2:15 PM
To: Madeline Whittaker <madeline@fivespoonspress.com>

I know we already talked last night about your big convo with Elliot, but I have one extra thought re: you thinking he's not as into this as you are because he doesn't always respond as fast as you'd like him to: Forgive me but why do I have a hunch that when I don't text/email you for a bit and then tell you it's because I've been busy, you believe me, but when Elliot (aka YOUR BOYFRIEND) doesn't respond in a timely fashion, you take it so personally?

You like him. And like most sane people, you don't like that many other people. But watch that your anxiety doesn't drive you to crazy town.

You know who else is normally too busy to press "reply" half the time? YOU. Find that bitch and put her to work.

Have fun at the Four Seasons.

x

Subject: Re: (no subject)
From: Madeline Whittaker <madeline@fivespoonspress.com>
Date: Mon, May 12 at 2:31 PM
To: Emily Roberts <emilyrobertshere@gmail.com>

"Find that bitch and put her to work."

Hearts to you.

Madeline

Hola. What time (approximately) do you want to meet tonight or drinks beforehand if u can? xoxo

May 15, 11:45 AM

Elliot

Hola! Working lunch shift today, so can come right after. Even brought overnight bag with me to work :)

May 15, 12:20 PM

Madeline

Me too! Awww. It's like we're running away from home. Let's meet at 5 in the hotel lobby x

May 15, 1:45 PM

Elliot

Pretty sure that's an R. Kelly lyric. Into it. See you there!

May 15, 3:40 PM

THE NEXT DAY...

Subject: Question!
From: Elliot Rowe <elliot@salatowest.com>
Date: Fri, May 16 at 2:45 PM
To: Madeline Whittaker <madeline@fivespoonspress.com>

Do you seriously think they're gonna charge me for this robe? You can't stock your hotel room with robes that soft and not expect people to take them. It's entrapment!

BTW—when I checked out, the lady at the concierge was like, "Did you and your girlfriend enjoy your stay?" Sounded nice. :)

Subject: Re: Question!
From: Madeline Whittaker <madeline@fivespoonspress.com>
Date: Fri, May 16 at 3:15 PM
To: Elliot Rowe <elliot@salatowest.com>

Ha! I think the robe is the one thing that they do charge you for, barring ripping a sconce off the wall. Yes, I said "sconce."

WELL. 4 out of 5 concierge ladies can't be wrong, can they?

P.S. Yes, the robe did look awesome (especially when tossed on a chair), though now my boss is going to think my Norwegian cookbook author is a robe thief and that is coming out of her budget. Just FY to the I. x

Subject: Re: Question!
From: Elliot Rowe <elliot@salatowest.com>
Date: Fri, May 16 at 4:22 PM
To: Madeline Whittaker <madeline@fivespoonspress.com>

Did we just get you fired? Please don't get fired—I'm fairly certain I don't make enough money to support us. And while I'm enjoying bf/gf status right now, I'm not sure that taking the next step and getting married to get us tax breaks is the right move just yet . . .

Subject: Re: Question!
From: Madeline Whittaker <madeline@fivespoonspress.com>
Date: Fri, May 16 at 4:52 PM
To: Elliot Rowe <elliot@salatowest.com>

Oh, no worries. I can get fired and we can live off the phat of the land. "The land" in this case being the stretch of grass when you come off the subway at Houston. Or a median barrier on Park Ave. I can forage for nuts and berries and pigeon meat and you can cook it. "The Median Food Movement." Boom: Styles section profile. Boom: Food truck. Boom: Triplex.

xo

Subject: Re: (no subject)
From: Emily Roberts <emilyrobertshere@gmail.com>
Date: Fri, May 16 at 8:30 PM
To: Madeline Whittaker <madeline@fivespoonspress.com>

So . . . how was it?

Subject: Re: (no subject)
From: Madeline Whittaker <madeline@fivespoonspress.com>
Date: Fri, May 16 at 8:58 PM
To: Emily Roberts <emilyrobertshere@gmail.com>

Okay, kind of amazing. We just played . . . well, we also had lots of
the sex. But we literally bounced on the bed and ordered room
service and prank called other rooms like 13-year-olds. Straight out
of a romantic comedy.

But a decent indie romantic comedy. It was just . . . easy. And
reminded me of why I like him so much.

It reminded me of the time my 19-year-old cat was dying. Stay
with me here: my mom called and I went home to say good-bye to
said cat and unfortunately got there the moment it died. So I had this
visual of a dead cat that overrode half my memories of the cat when
it was alive. Last night was like a dead cat . . . in a good way, in that
it overrode 80% of my insecurities. I know they are there. Just like I
remember the cat when it was alive and kicking. Follow me?

Conclusion: he is the dead cat of my dreams.

He did, annoyingly, steal a bathrobe from the room though. And
I will, equally annoyingly, have to explain that. I think he genuinely
thought the Four Seasons wouldn't notice. They charge for WiFi in
the lobby. They'll notice.

Subject: Re: (no subject)
From: Emily Roberts <emilyrobertshere@gmail.com>
Date: Fri, May 16 at 9:08 PM
To: Madeline Whittaker <madeline@fivespoonspress.com>

Oh hey, remember that time you compared your relationship to a dead cat? Hahahaha.

Honestly, psyched for you. I think you guys are actually maybe good for each other after all I love to see you all beam-y. Even if it's weird Madeline beam-y.

Um . . . but also? WHO THE FUCK STEALS THE ROBE? Has he never stayed in a hotel before? Is he a homeless chimney sweep? Hope you don't get in trouble.

Subject: Re: (no subject)
From: Madeline Whittaker <madeline@fivespoonspress.com>
Date: Fri, May 16 at 9:15 PM
To: Emily Roberts <emilyrobertshere@gmail.com>

Seriously, I skip off to work and leave him in the room (all very reverse "Pretty Woman") and that's what he tells me. Most of his friends are kind of high-functioning wastrels, so maybe it's normal behavior for them. Who knows.

Actually that's not entirely true—his lawyer friend David is alright. You guys should meet at some point.

Subject: Re: (no subject)
From: Emily Roberts <emilyrobertshere@gmail.com>
Date: Fri, May 16 at 9:20 PM
To: Madeline Whittaker <madeline@fivespoonspress.com>

Wow. A bunch of "high-functioning wastrels" and a guy who's "alright." I guess my Mojave dry spell continues on.

xo

Subject: (no subject)
From: Elliot Rowe <elliot@salatowest.com>
Date: Sat, May 17 at 11:06 AM
To: David Meyer <davidmeyer@lathamlaw.com>

Holy shit.

You will never guess who I just ran into.

Subject: Re: (no subject)
From: David Meyer <davidmeyer@lathamlaw.com>
Date: Sat, May 17 at 11:43 AM
To: Elliot Rowe <elliot@salatowest.com>

Anna Kendrick??

Subject: Re: (no subject)
From: Elliot Rowe <elliot@salatowest.com>
Date: Sat, May 17 at 11:48 AM
To: David Meyer <davidmeyer@lathamlaw.com>

What? No . . . Ellie.

Why would I have run into Anna Kendrick?

Subject: Re: (no subject)
From: David Meyer <davidmeyer@lathamlaw.com>
Date: Sat, May 17 at 11:49 AM
To: Elliot Rowe <elliot@salatowest.com>

Just saw on TMZ that she's filming a movie right around the corner from your apt. Wishful thinking.

Ellie is way less exciting. She probably can't even do the "Cups" song. What happened?

Subject: Re: (no subject)
From: Elliot Rowe <elliot@salatowest.com>
Date: Sat, May 17 at 11:51 AM
To: David Meyer <davidmeyer@lathamlaw.com>

So I'm grabbing coffee at Bluebird, still recooperating from the Four Seasons, when who do I see tied up outside? Iggy. I was actually gonna leave because I didn't really feel like doing a whole song and dance when she came out.

We only spoke for like two secs—she said she was on her way to go style some shoot (couldn't tell if she actually was or whether she was lying to appear busy)—but she texted me this right after:

"Good seeing you . . . Was actually just talking about you with my therapist. Go figure. :) "

Subject: Re: (no subject)
From: David Meyer <davidmeyer@lathamlaw.com>
Date: Sat, May 17 at 11:55 AM
To: Elliot Rowe <elliot@salatowest.com>

LOL. "Just talking about you with my therapist." Equal parts casual, intimate, funny, unsettling, and intriguing, all in an economical seven words. That is classic Ellie right there. Does she knows you're seeing someone?

Subject: Re: (no subject)
From: Elliot Rowe <elliot@salatowest.com>
Date: Sat, May 17 at 11:57 AM
To: David Meyer <davidmeyer@lathamlaw.com>

She still follows me on Instagram so I'm sure she has some idea.

She also said she's gonna be at Hayley and Justin's wedding . . .

Subject: Re: (no subject)
From: David Meyer <davidmeyer@lathamlaw.com>
Date: Sat, May 17 at 11:58 AM
To: Elliot Rowe <elliot@salatowest.com>

Are you taking Madeline to that?

Subject: Re: (no subject)
From: Elliot Rowe <elliot@salatowest.com>
Date: Sat, May 17 at 12:02 PM
To: David Meyer <davidmeyer@lathamlaw.com>

It's weird—Ellie was invited as my plus one, but obviously she's good friends with them too, so she's still going. But I don't know if that means I get a *different* +1. This etiquette is very complicated.
     Guess I should ask Justin . . .

Subject: Re: (no subject)
From: Elliot Rowe <elliot@salatowest.com>
Date: Sat, May 17 at 4:06 PM
To: David Meyer <davidmeyer@lathamlaw.com>

Justin said it's cool if I bring someone, but that Ellie's coming solo.

Huh.

Subject: Re: (no subject)
From: David Meyer <davidmeyer@lathamlaw.com>
Date: Sat, May 17 at 4:15 PM
To: Elliot Rowe <elliot@salatowest.com>

Well if Ellie *was* bringing someone, I have no doubt you'd be bringing Madeline. But since she's not, now you don't know?

Subject: Re: (no subject)
From: Elliot Rowe <elliot@salatowest.com>
Date: Sat, May 17 at 4:24 PM
To: David Meyer <davidmeyer@lathamlaw.com>

Okay, it's not like I want to go solo up there. I just don't know if the stress of bringing Madeline is worth it. She won't know anyone there, and it's still pretty new. Just doesn't feel like it'll be fun for anyone.

Subject: Re: (no subject}
From: David Meyer <davidmeyer@lathamlaw.com>
Date: Sat, May 17 at 4:27 PM
To: Elliot Rowe <elliot@salatowest.com>

Got it.

Subject: Re: (no subject)
From: Elliot Rowe <elliot@salatowest.com>
Date: Sat, May 17 at 4:35 PM
To: David Meyer <davidmeyer@lathamlaw.com>

Don't say "got it" like that. I can feel your judgement through my iphone screen.

Subject: Re: (no subject)
From: David Meyer <davidmeyer@lathamlaw.com>
Date: Sat, May 17 at 4:40 PM
To: Elliot Rowe <elliot@salatowest.com>

I wasn't saying "got it" sarcastically, as if I don't believe that even on a subconscious level you have no desire to be in an intimate, rural environment with lots of alcohol with your ex-girlfriend who just said she was thinking about you. I meant "got it" in that I genuinely believe it would be stressful to have Madeline there. But I'm glad you're not defensive or anything.

Subject: Re: (no subject)
From: Elliot Rowe <elliot@salatowest.com>
Date: Sat, May 17 at 4:42 PM
To: David Meyer <davidmeyer@lathamlaw.com>

Oh.

Got it.

I think I just need a little time to clear my head. A lot to process right now.

Madeline

Hey Hey! What are you/we up to this fine eve?

May 18, 6:18 PM

Elliot

hey hey—actually, not feeling so hot, so probably not a whole lot. :/ What about you?

May 18, 7:02 PM

Madeline

Hmm . . . not sure.

May 18, 7:04 PM

Sorry you're not feeling so hot. I am not the chef in this conversation but I do know how to buy soup . . .

May 18, 7:05 PM

Elliot

Oh that's sweet but don't worry—I think its regular-sick not lupus-sick. Though it would be kind of crazy if I had lupus. Do people even get lupus anymore?

May 18, 7:17 PM

I should check WebMD for lupus symptoms.

May 18, 7:18 PM

Madeline

Well, you get a skin rash with lupus so let's hope you don't have that. It's not like diphtheria. It's a thing that still happens.

Just text me later. take it easy, k? x

May 18, 7:18 PM

A FEW DAYS LATER...

Subject: Re: Question!
From: Elliot Rowe <elliot@salatowest.com>
Date: Wed, May 21 at 5:43 PM
To: Madeline Whittaker <madeline@fivespoonspress.com>

Hey Hey,

I know we were supposed to hang tonight but mind if I just crash at my place? Still feeling a little under the weather—and like one more bad night's sleep won't help things.

Let's catch up this wknd.

--------Forwarded Message-------
Subject: Re: Question!
From: Elliot Rowe <elliot@salatowest.com>
Date: Wed, May 21 at 5:43 PM
To: Madeline Whittaker <madeline@fivespoonspress.com>

Hey Hey,

I know we were supposed to hang tonight but mind if I just crash at . . .

Subject: [Fwd: Re: Question!]
From: Madeline Whittaker <madeline@fivespoonspress.com>
Date: Wed, May 21 at 5:50 PM
To: Emily Roberts <emilyrobertshere@gmail.com>

Umm. What is happening all of a sudden? Highlights include but are
not limited to:

• Suddenly we need to "catch up" this weekend? What? Should we
also "reconvene" while we're at it?
• We've spoken in between this but still. Feeling funky. Am I crazy to
feel funky?
• End of bullet points, start of ice-cream smoking and cigarette eating.

Subject: Re: [Fwd: Re: Question!]
From: Emily Roberts <emilyrobertshere@gmail.com>
Date: Wed, May 21 at 6:30 PM
To: Madeline Whittaker <madeline@fivespoonspress.com>

Okay. You're not crazy. This is weird. And right on the heels of Barbie's DreamHotel Sexfest™.
  I don't know what to tell you. Except that boys need their space? How are you feeling about it now?

x

Subject: Re: [Fwd: Re: Question!]
From: Madeline Whittaker <madeline@fivespoonspress.com>
Date: Wed, May 21 at 6:33 PM
To: Emily Roberts <emilyrobertshere@gmail.com>

Not great! I mean, do I require that he refer to our sex life as "making love"? No. But I'm a little insulted that he'd categorize it as a "bad night's sleep." Oh, I'm sorry . . . are the blow jobs an inconvenience for you?
  I have no idea how to respond to this.

Subject: Re: [Fwd: Re: Question!]
From: Emily Roberts <emilyrobertshere@gmail.com>
Date: Wed, May 21 at 6:37 PM
To: Madeline Whittaker <madeline@fivespoonspress.com>

"Are the blow jobs an inconvenience for you?" . . . seems like a solid choice.
  No, really, if you can muster up something a little less angry than that (all i know is do NOT be angry . . . you're not married . . . relationships at this juncture are volunteer positions.)
  Keep it short and simple and breezy. Something you won't regret in case.

Subject: Re: [Fwd: Re: Question!]
From: Madeline Whittaker <madeline@fivespoonspress.com>
Date: Wed, May 21 at 6:37 PM
To: Emily Roberts <emilyrobertshere@gmail.com>

IN CASE OF WHAT?

Subject: Re: [Fwd: Re: Question!]
From: Emily Roberts <emilyrobertshere@gmail.com>
Date: Wed, May 21 at 6:40 PM
To: Madeline Whittaker <madeline@fivespoonspress.com>

LADY:
  You know in "What About Bob?" when Bill Murray has to "take a vacation from my problems"? Take some space for you while he's taking some space for him. Tell him no worries. And then . . . actually don't worry.
  Baby steps out of the apartment.

E x

Subject: Re: [Fwd: Re: Question!]
From: Madeline Whittaker <madeline@fivespoonspress.com>
Date: Wed, May 21 at 6:43 PM
To: Emily Roberts <emilyrobertshere@gmail.com>

Yeah, I know it. It's funny . . . suddenly everyone we know is getting married and able to spell "boutonniere" when they couldn't do it yesterday—and I think when Elliot and I joke about it, has this "us" vs. "them" effect. "Us" is the entity that thinks commitment is silly. "We" aren't like that! "We" are chill! "We" have icicles for hearts! "Them," on the other hand, are the morons who think they can see forever. Who introduce people to their families too quickly. Who can't foresee the end of everything despite the fact that THERE HASN'T BEEN A CIVILIZATION ON EARTH, EVER, THAT HASN'T CRUMBLED.

Anyway I am a combination of "us" and "them." I don't wake up seeing forever but I also acknowledge it as a real destination.

I guess it's all a roundabout way of saying that I feel like there's something here and I don't want to lose it. On the other hand, I don't want to be made the chump because I had the audacity to hope (thanks, Obama).

xo

P.S. Thanks for listening. You're good at this, you know?

Subject: Re: [Fwd: Re: Question!]
From: Emily Roberts <emilyrobertshere@gmail.com>
Date: Wed, May 21 at 7:15 PM
To: Madeline Whittaker <madeline@fivespoonspress.com>

I think the best thing I can do for you now is tell you to not indulge in this.

THINK ABOUT ANYTHING ELSE. He sure as shit is.

x

P.S. Don't be weird. Respond to his email but be breezy and brief. You won't regret saying less right now.

P.P.S. You would be good at this too if you spent your days settling pushing fights between 7-year-olds.

Subject: Re: Question!
From: Madeline Whittaker <madeline@fivespoonspress.com>
Date: Wed, May 21 at 7:30 PM
To: Elliot Rowe <elliot@salatowest.com>

Hey hey back—

Of course not. Totally understand. See you this weekend.

A FEW DAYS LATER...

Subject: Hey!
From: Elliot Rowe <elliot@salatowest.com>
Date: Sat, May 24 at 4:45 PM
To: Madeline Whittaker <madeline@fivespoonspress.com>

hiiiiiii,

feeling slightly human again. thank god I quarantined myself and limited the number of people I potentially got sick to the Thai delivery guy (don't worry I tipped extra). What are you up to tonight?

Subject: Re: Hey!
From: Madeline Whittaker <madeline@fivespoonspress.com>
Date: Sat, May 24 at 5:06 PM
To: Elliot Rowe <elliot@salatowest.com>

Glad you're back in fighting form. What am I doing tonight? Umm . . . something fun with you? We can do whatever but also maybe meet up with Emily and some of my friends at some point?

Madeline

Subject: Re: Hey!
From: Elliot Rowe <elliot@salatowest.com>
Date: Sat, May 24 at 5:15 PM
To: Madeline Whittaker <madeline@fivespoonspress.com>

Sounds good. Don't think Imma be staying out too late tonight, but maybe something low-key like drinks and a movie? Can check what's playing and get back to ya.

Maybe can meet up with Emily and friends after, or leave you chicks to it . . .

Subject: Re: Hey!
From: Madeline Whittaker <madeline@fivespoonspress.com>
Date: Sat, May 24 at 5:24 PM
To: Elliot Rowe <elliot@salatowest.com>

"Chicks." We don't speak in clucks and leave feathers everywhere.

Anyway, don't want to drag you out of the house if you're still sick. Especially out of the house and into a public movie theater (you've seen "Outbreak," yeah?). So whatever is fine w/ me.

--------Forwarded Message-------
Subject: Re: Hey!
From: Madeline Whittaker <madeline@fivespoonspress.com>
Date: Sat, May 24 at 5:06 PM
To: Elliot Rowe <elliot@salatowest.com>

Glad you're back in fighting form. What am I doing tonight? Umm . . .

Subject: Hey!
From: Elliot Rowe <elliot@salatowest.com>
Date: Sat, May 24 at 4:45 PM
To: Madeline Whittaker <madeline@fivespoonspress.com>

hiiiiiii,
    feeling slightly human again. thank god I quarantined myself . . .

Subject: [Fwd: Re: Hey!]
From: Madeline Whittaker <madeline@fivespoonspress.com>
Date: Sat, May 24 at 5:29 PM
To: Emily Roberts <emilyrobertshere@gmail.com>

Note the "hiiiiii." So. Many. Vowels.

Subject: Re: [Fwd: Re: Hey!]
From: Emily Roberts <emilyrobertshere@gmail.com>
Date: Sat, May 24 at 5:40 PM
To: Madeline Whittaker <madeline@fivespoonspress.com>

Aww, see? Everything's fine. He's a human! Humans need rest.

See you both soon. I guess.

Subject: Re: [Fwd: Re: Hey!]
From: Madeline Whittaker <madeline@fivespoonspress.com>
Date: Sat, May 24 at 5:52 PM
To: Emily Roberts <emilyrobertshere@gmail.com>

I know. I just feel weirdly vulnerable all of a sudden. Case in point: He says he'll look up show times for a movie and it's as if he just sent me flowers.

Subject: Re: [Fwd: Re: Hey!]
From: Emily Roberts <emilyrobertshere@gmail.com>
Date: Sat, May 24 at 5:59 PM
To: Madeline Whittaker <madeline@fivespoonspress.com>

Madeline, you are the biggest book geek I know. Are you really getting this bent out of shape over someone who unironically employs the phrase "Imma be"? I know, I know, Elliot is soooo funny and sooo smart and has street sense coming out his ears. But you know what's on the street? The Strand. Go read a book, dude.

Sorry, I'm PMSing, hate everyone today and come bearing an emotional wiffle ball bat.

xo

Subject: Re: [Fwd: Re: Hey!]
From: Madeline Whittaker <madeline@fivespoonspress.com>
Date: Sat, May 24 at 6:15 PM
To: Emily Roberts <emilyrobertshere@gmail.com>

A) I love you. B) Imma c u l8r.

Subject: Re: [Fwd: Re: Hey!]
From: Emily Roberts <emilyrobertshere@gmail.com>
Date: Sun, May 25 at 10:04 AM
To: Madeline Whittaker <madeline@fivespoonspress.com>

How are you doing? Sorry we didn't meet up last night. All good with Elliot, though? x

---

Subject: Re: [Fwd: Re: Hey!]
From: Madeline Whittaker <madeline@fivespoonspress.com>
Date: Sun, May 25 at 10:15 AM
To: Emily Roberts <emilyrobertshere@gmail.com>

Morning,
   I am good. I'm fine. More importantly: How are you?
   Oh hey, guess what? Turns out Elliot will be away in a couple of weeks. For work, you ask? For a funeral? For a frontal lobotomy? Nope: for a wedding on a sprawling romantic goat farm in Vermont. One of his bffs from college. Never even occurred to him to invite me. He just announced it like you might announce a dentist appt.
   To play devil's advocate: it's a wedding. Kind of unfair to ask people who you've never even met to pay an extra hundred bucks to cover their old pal's new girlfriend. Still . . .

Subject: Re: [Fwd: Re: Hey!]
From: Emily Roberts <emilyrobertshere@gmail.com>
Date: Sun, May 25 at 10:45 AM
To: Madeline Whittaker <madeline@fivespoonspress.com>

I'm sure that's it. Believe me, there's plenty of things I think you should take personally. But this isn't one of them.
   And I am good! A 3rd-grader threw up on my shoes this week. x

---

Elliot

Just wanted to say sorry again that this whole invite situation was such a clusterfuck. I want you to come, but totally get the whole last-minute thing.

May 25, 12:30 PM

Madeline

Last minute as in you're inviting me last minute? Sorry, I didn't fully get that I was being invited. But no worries. It's a wedding and timing really isn't the issue so much as asking your old friend for a +1 . . .

May 25, 1:45 PM

I think +1s are generally reserved for +2 year relationships . . . have fun without me. x

May 25, 1:50 PM

SAVE the DATE

♥

Hayley Cooper & Justin Levy
—— Saturday, June 14th ——
Berkshire, Vermont

JUNE

Subject: Greetings from Vermont!
From: Elliot Rowe <elliot@salatowest.com>
Date: Thu, Jun 12 at 6:15 PM
To: Madeline Whittaker <madeline@fivespoonspress.com>

Just got here. Cell reception kinda spotty but will try to call when
I get a sec . . .
　　Has NY changed drastically since I left??

xx

Subject: Re: Greetings from Vermont!
From: Madeline Whittaker <madeline@fivespoonspress.com>
Date: Thu, Jun 12 at 8:08 PM
To: Elliot Rowe <elliot@salatowest.com>

I don't think New York has changed too much. I mean . . . is everyone
having threesomes and doing blow off the sidewalk? Sure, that.
　　Headed out into the mean streets of the West Village tonight for
some party in some friend of Emily's apartment.

Milk a goat for me,

M

Subject: Re: Greetings from Vermont!
From: Elliot Rowe <elliot@salatowest.com>
Date: Thu, Jun 12 at 8:10 PM
To: Madeline Whittaker <madeline@fivespoonspress.com>

That shouldn't be hard, little guys are just chillin' all over the property. Pretty awesome.

 Running off to the rehearsal dinner, will try to call after. xx

---

Subject: Re: Greetings from Vermont!
From: Madeline Whittaker <madeline@fivespoonspress.com>
Date: Thu, Jun 12 at 8:48 PM
To: Elliot Rowe <elliot@salatowest.com>

Sounds good. Have fun!

Subject: (no subject)
From: David Meyer <davidmeyer@lathamlaw.com>
Date: Fri, Jun 13 at 11:45 AM
To: Elliot Rowe <elliot@salatowest.com>

I think we as a society need to re-examine this whole "wedding hashtag" phenomenon. I don't need to see a picture of the #LevyPartyfor2 table centerpiece from everyone with a goddamn iPhone.

How's Ellie? Just an FYI, I will regretfully be "unable to attend" if #ElliotandEllie is rekindled.

Subject: Re: (no subject)
From: Elliot Rowe <elliot@salatowest.com>
Date: Fri. Jun 13 at 12:09 PM
To: David Meyer <davidmeyer@lathamlaw.com>

I don't think you'll have to worry about that. Last night, she was running around in a short skirt and heels even though we're in a field in fucking Vermont and it's cold out at night and it all just felt . . . old. I dunno. Towards the end of the night she kept saying how great it was to catch up and how she hadn't been dating because she was trying to "work on herself right now," and I could tell she wanted me to make a move and literally the whole time I was just thinking, "I wish Madeline was here, I wish Madeline was here." Dunno what I was thinking not inviting her.

Then I ended up smoking a bunch of cigarettes, so it was pretty much a loss on all counts.

Subject: (no subject)
From: Madeline Whittaker <madeline@fivespoonspress.com>
Date: Fri, Jun 13 at 1:06 PM
To: Emily Roberts <emilyrobertshere@gmail.com>

HOLY SHIT BALLS!

His ex is there. And *of course* he's said nothing and *of course* that's exactly why he didn't invite me to begin with.

Wtf?

Subject: Re: (no subject)
From: Emily Roberts <emilyrobertshere@gmail.com>
Date: Fri, Jun 13 at 1:32 PM
To: Madeline Whittaker <madeline@fivespoonspress.com>

Wait . . . How do you know this?

Subject: Re: (no subject)
From: Madeline Whittaker <madeline@fivespoonspress.com>
Date: Fri, Jun 13 at 1:45 PM
To: Emily Roberts <emilyrobertshere@gmail.com>

Because Elliot's friends have public Instagram feeds and I went down the rabbit hole . . . I did this until I stumbled across an actual hash tag for the wedding.

Anyway, one click got me pics from all sorts of randos, including 2-3 flashes of a blonde who is CLEARLY Elliot's ex (oh, and to answer your question before you ask it: Facebook and prior Google Image search after the first night we met . . . that's how). In one of the bride and groom dancing, she's chatting with him in the background. She's a living nightmare named "Ellie." I can send it to you. You can analyze their body language for me . . .

Subject: Re: (no subject)
From: Emily Roberts <emilyrobertshere@gmail.com>
Date: Fri, Jun 13 at 2:45 PM
To: Madeline Whittaker <madeline@fivespoonspress.com>

Ummm . . . don't do that. I love you but I don't need to see that.

   Listen, maybe he didn't invite you because his ex was there and he thought it would be weird. Was he really going to tell you that???

   He hasn't done anything wrong . . . yet. I think you should wait and see how he handles it upon his return. See if he mentions it or not . . . I think it might be a little weird if he doesn't mention it.

   Either way two things:

   1. Step away from the tiny screen
   2. Leave the house
   3. Ellie is a dumb name

   (apparently I can teach my kids to number things but I can't count things)

E x

Subject: Re: Greetings from Vermont!
Subject: Re: Greetings from Vermont!
From: Elliot Rowe <elliot@salatowest.com>
Date: Fri, Jun 13, 9:54 PM
To: Madeline Whittaker <madeline@fivespoonspress.com>

Heyyy. You get my vmail? Will try again later tonight. xx

Subject: Re: Greetings from Vermont!
From: Elliot Rowe <elliot@salatowest.com>
Date: Sat, Jun 14 at 10:06 AM
To: Madeline Whittaker <madeline@fivespoonspress.com>

Morning! Guess I missed you last night. Extremely hungover but slowly recuperating with a bacon, egg, and cheese sandwich, all components of which were made on premise. Very literally farm to table.

Bunch of us are gonna go on some sort of "nature walk," which I guess is what they call hikes here. Will try you again before the wedding. Still can't believe we have to actually drink at that. Talk soon.

Subject: Re: (no subject)
From: Madeline Whittaker <madeline@fivespoonspress.com>
Date: Sat, Jun 14 at 11:06 AM
To: Emily Roberts <emilyrobertshere@gmail.com>

Hey,

Just tried to call you. You're probably still sleeping. I *could* wait for you to call me back but this story is burning a hole in my pocket.

Okay (rolls up sleeves): as per your advice, I did "take a night" for myself. But it would take a more psychologically stable person than myself to stay home, knowing Elliot was probably out gallivanting with this Ellie person.

When I left the house last night, all I could think was: "Maybe Elliot and I are only good in a bubble." Only good in a suite at the Four Seasons. I started thinking . . . okay, we've met some of each other's friends but if this relationship is happening in isolation, it's going to be pretty easy to throw it away without consequence. This is what's floating around my head when I leave the house.

So. . . I go out to dinner with a friend from work and her husband, which feels like maybe the exact wrong thing to do, to sit across from a well-defined couple. I am running late and when I get there, it's my friend, her husband, and a jacket slung over an empty chair. And unless some mystery female guest is subscribing to the menswear trend a little too hard, I deduce that a person with a penis will be joining us. These are the real consequences of living your relationship in a bubble: a reasonably good friend, whom I've sat down the hall from for years, thinks I'm in a position to be set up on a date.

Then the guy emerges from the bathroom.

His name is Jared and he has numerous artfully arranged Tibetan scarves around his neck, ripped T-shirt and the ethnic charms hanging from leather cords . . . he may as well have had a button that read "Ask Me About My Charm Necklaces!" And yet . . . he is hot.

Anyway, we have a perfectly nice time and the food is fine (since dating Elliot, I've become a restaurant snob . . .), but not great and so Jared and I begin to drink.

After dinner, we hit a bar across the way and Jared is being REALLY flattering. He's telling me I'm some holy trifecta of clever and sophisticated and sexy. And because I've recently become accustomed to Elliot's scraps, to noting when his texts don't say "xx" . . . I fell for it.

Suddenly my friend and her husband cut out, 'cause obviously there's been a pow wow I have not been privy to. And about six seconds later, Jared leans over and kisses me. And I kiss him back. And we are basically mugging down in the bar and it's strange and guilt-inducing so I disengage. Then he's like "do you live near here?" And that's when I pulled the plug. Still . . . that happened.

Subject: Re: (no subject)
From: Emily Roberts <emilyrobertshere@gmail.com>
Date: Sat, Jun 14 at 12:02 PM
To: Madeline Whittaker <madeline@fivespoonspress.com>

Whoa. Holy boy drama Batman.

You want to know what I did last night? I met my sister and nieces for dinner, and sat at the worst "pub" bar ever (your newly refined food snob might take issue with cold mozzarella sticks) while my sister could literally not complete one sentence without either answering my nieces' questions or addressing them—"Are you enjoying Mommy's cheese stick?"

Then I went home, vacuumed, read 1/4th of a Talk of the Town piece, and passed out. Meanwhile, across town . . .

Are you going to tell Elliot? Because I don't think you should? In fact, I am going to skip the judgment and ask the hard questions: You made out with a guy with a Tibetan neck scarf? It's like I don't even know you anymore.

Subject: Re: (no subject)
From: Madeline Whittaker <madeline@fivespoonspress.com>
Date: Sat, Jun 14 at 12:08 PM
To: Emily Roberts <emilyrobertshere@gmail.com>

Would it help if I told you it was a locally sourced Tibetan scarf and all the proceeds go to clean drinking water?

Subject: Re: (no subject)
From: Emily Roberts <emilyrobertshere@gmail.com>
Date: Sat, Jun 14 at 12:12 PM
To: Madeline Whittaker <madeline@fivespoonspress.com>

Probably not since the reason you know that is because this dude made sure you knew it . . . right before he stuck his tongue down your throat.

Elliot

I am so fucking hungover and Madeline is being really weird and evasive. Great weekend all around!

Jun 15, 10:45 AM

David

Just got out of hot yoga. Feeling pretty #blessed actually.

Jun 15, 11:04 AM

You seeing her tonight?

Jun 15, 11:06 AM

Elliot

If she ever responds to me.

Jun 15, 11:12 AM

David

I'm sure she will.

Jun 15, 11:15 AM

Actually I take that back. Maybe she won't. This whole thing is kind of a shit show.

Jun 15, 11:16 AM

Have a safe ride home!

Jun 15, 11:24 AM

Subject: Re: Greetings from Vermont!
From: Elliot Rowe <elliot@salatowest.com>
Date: Sun, Jun 15 at 12:02 PM
To: Madeline Whittaker <madeline@fivespoonspress.com>

Earrrrrth to Madeline?

Getting hungover self to car and driving hungover self back to the city and attempting not to vomit tequila all over this rental in the process. Not sure where you are, but would like to cuddle up with your (presumably less hungover) self tonight . . . Be back in like 5 hrs.

xx

Subject: Re: Greetings from Vermont!
From: Madeline Whittaker <madeline@fivespoonspress.com>
Date: Sun, Jun 15 at 1:45 PM
To: Elliot Rowe <elliot@salatowest.com>

Hey!

Sorry, it's been kind of a crazy weekend. Had to go into the office (fun) but then, in an effort to squeeze the most out of my weekend, wound up going out pretty late Friday night and then deciding it was a wise choice to do the whole thing all over again on Saturday night. So that's where I'm at mental-capacity-wise.

I'll text you in a bit. Looking forward to hearing a play-by-play of this wedding spectacular . . .

M x

P.S. I'm more of a table-to-farm girl myself. Trying to think of the matching joke: Something having to do with chucking silverware into a field.

Madeline

So . . . he came clean about the wedding. All my paranoia for naught. (Pretty glad I let the Jared thing fade.)

Jun 16, 10:02 AM

Emily

Good boy! That must feel good.

Jun 16, 10:30 AM

Madeline

Yup. All good.

Jun 16, 10:45 AM

Emily

Heh. You type like a dude when you're happy.

Jun 16, 10:52 AM

Subject: 101
From: David Meyer <davidmeyer@lathamlaw.com>
Date: Mon, Jun 16 at 10:05 AM
To: Elliot Rowe <elliot@salatowest.com>

"Elliot Rowe and Madeline Whittaker are now in a Relationship."
Thought this was old news but glad you're making it Facebook
official. Also you're a huge dork. I take it she got over your non-invite
invite?

Subject: Re: 101
From: Elliot Rowe <elliot@salatowest.com>
Date: Mon, Jun 16 at 10:45 AM
To: David Meyer <davidmeyer@lathamlaw.com>

Calm down we did it as a joke (but you better "like" it).
  And yes, she did. Basically, I just told her that I spent the whole
weekend wishing she was there and that the only reason I didn't
push harder for her to come was because I didn't want her to have
to deal with any Ellie drama. But that seeing Ellie there made me
realize how over the whole thing I was, and made me excited to
come back and see her. And she was like, "Yeah, I actually knew
Ellie was there, I saw her in a bunch of Instagram photos." haha.
So it's a good thing I brought it up first.
  What are you up to Thursday? Wanna come by the restaurant? We
got a bunch of whole ducks in from Pennsylvania that are gonna be
delicious. Madeline's coming with Emily. Who is still single.

Subject: Re: 101
From: David Meyer <davidmeyer@lathamlaw.com>
Date: Mon, Jun 16 at 10:56 AM
To: Elliot Rowe <elliot@salatowest.com>

Love duck, but supposed to get drinks with this girl (pic attached). Could come by after.

    I actually like Emily a lot, though not sure how much she likes me. I always feel like she's judging me. Probably the whole teacher thing.

Subject: Re: 101
From: Elliot Rowe <elliot@salatowest.com>
Date: Mon, Jun 16 at 11:00 AM
To: David Meyer <davidmeyer@lathamlaw.com>

This girl looks like she could be a hostess at an Asian fusion restaurant in Vegas, but not actually old enough to drink there.

    I wonder why Emily would judge you?

Subject: (no subject)
From: Elliot Rowe <elliot@salatowest.com>
Date: Thu, Jun 19 at 2:45 PM
To: Madeline Whittaker <madeline@fivespoonspress.com>

Looks like we tapped out at 57 likes, 42 of which are from people I haven't talked to in at least 18 months.

Don't really know what to make of that number, as a photo of my grandma playing golf in Scottsdale over Christmas got 86 likes. Either way, excited for tonight!

Subject: Re: (no subject)
From: Madeline Whittaker <madeline@fivespoonspress.com>
Date: Thu, Jun 19 at 3:06 PM
To: Elliot Rowe <elliot@salatowest.com>

Wouldn't read too much into it—old people kill it on Facebook. Old people, cats, and babies. Especially Japanese babies, which are basically the cutest living things on the planet. I basically think all babies should be born Japanese and then some stay because, hey, you gotta have Japanese people. Uh, anyway . . .

Excited for tonight, too! Mostly to meet David's barely legal date. Related: We need to find Emily a dude. Keep your eyes open.

Off to an author lunch where I will try to eat lightly in preparation for duck.

xoxox M

Elliot

What do you think would happen if we just left David, Emily, and Tricia alone at this table together?

Jun 19, 10:06 PM

Madeline

Fuck Tricia, marry Emily, kill David. Oh wait, wrong game.

Jun 19, 10:07 PM

Mistake #1: Leaving Emily alone with a stripper (?) in a room full of knives

Jun 19, 10:07 PM

Elliot

It was Emily in the kitchen with the steak knife!

Jun 19, 10:11 PM

Oh, wait, wrong game.

Jun 19, 10:11 PM

Not a stripper btw. "Pharmaceutical sales rep." Though I think a Venn Diagram between the two would have a lot of overlap.

Jun 19, 10:12 PM

Madeline

I would like to Venn your Diagram.

Jun 19, 10:31 PM

Will you still make out with me even though I just make that joke? It was really bad.

Jun 19, 10:32 PM

Too bad one can't delete ducking texts.

Jun 19, 10:32 PM

ducking.

Jun 19, 10:32 PM

Fucking. Agggg. Stupid iPhone. I have never once meant "ducking." Also I'm drunk.

Jun 19, 10:32 PM

Elliot

I'd like to go home and take advantage of you please.

Jun 19, 11:08 PM

It's not taking advantage if I know about it ahead of time . . . and am in agreement. Of course, now I just have to leave Emily. She's been shooting me eye daggers for playing w/ my phone this whole time and I just looked up and mouthed "work."

Jun 19, 11:11 PM

Elliot

bad friend. Let's go . . . :)

Jun 19, 11:14 PM

Subject: Merci
From: Madeline Whittaker <madeline@fivespoonspress.com>
Date: Fri, Jun 20 at 8:45 AM
To: Emily Roberts <emilyrobertshere@gmail.com>

. . . thanks for coming last night. Do I owe you one? Why do I feel like I owe you one?

KISSES.

Subject: Re: Merci
From: Emily Roberts <emilyrobertshere@gmail.com>
Date: Fri, Jun 20 at 12:30 PM
To: Madeline Whittaker <madeline@fivespoonspress.com>

You owe me more than one. Or one very big one. WHO WAS THAT
SKANK? You know how I hate to turn on our own kind but . . .
At one point while you were making cooking-sex-face ("Oh, is that
how you whip vanilla beans into cream? Go faster, Elliot . . .") I got
trapped talking to David and that girl. Is she an actual stripper? You
know she showed me what was in her pocket at one point and I was
100% prepared for her to whip out a sex toy and instead she was
like: HERE'S THE PINK LEATHER-BOUND BIBLE I CARRY WITH ME
EVERYWHERE I GO.
   Whatever. I shall recover from one night of vapid conversation but
it's a shame because . . . I don't really know David well enough to
say that he could do better but isn't he a lawyer or something? He is
kind of cool and vaguely non-heinous-looking. Too bad he and Fluffy
the Bible Thumper had their hands down each other's pants (IN A
KITCHEN WITH AN "A" FROM THE DEPT. OF HEALTH, NO LESS).

I am dying laughing.

David

Full disclosure: I had sex with Tricia in the bathroom of your restaurant last night.

Jun 20, 10:02 AM

Elliot

Perfect. Does this mean Madeline and I can come have sex in the bathroom of your place of employ?

Jun 20, 10:22 AM

David

We actually have really spacious bathrooms here so be my guest.

Jun 20, 10:54 AM

Emily is pretty cool btw. Potentially too much of a real person for me right now, but when I'm looking for something serious in the next 8-10 years, I would like to revisit that.

Jun 20, 10:55 AM

Elliot

I will be sure to relay that information.

Jun 20, 11:22 PM

ONE WEEK LATER...

Subject: (no subject)
From: Madeline Whittaker <madeline@fivespoonspress.com>
Date: Sun, Jun 29 at 7:23 PM
To: Elliot Rowe <elliot@salatowest.com>

Hey, so just got an email from MOMA (I'm a member) and it looks like that Matisse exhibit, which is supposed to be great, closes next week. Should we go get our culture on this Saturday??

Subject: Re: (no subject)
From: Elliot Rowe <elliot@salatowest.com>
Date: Sun, Jun 29 at 8:15 PM
To: Madeline Whittaker <madeline@fivespoonspress.com>

A chance to put that art history class I took in college to use! But can't do Saturday—working lunch shift . . .

Subject: Re: (no subject)
From: Madeline Whittaker <madeline@fivespoonspress.com>
Date: Sun, Jun 29 at 8:34 PM
To: Elliot Rowe <elliot@salatowest.com>

Ah, bummer.
    I have a work dinner Tues (blah) and then a coworker birthday Wednesday (more blah), but free tomorrow. Let me know what your schedule's like this week.

Subject: Re: (no subject)
From: Elliot Rowe <elliot@salatowest.com>
Date: Sun, Jun 29 at 10:34 PM
To: Madeline Whittaker <madeline@fivespoonspress.com>

Do you mean for MOMA or for just hanging out in general?

Subject: Re: (no subject)
From: Madeline Whittaker <madeline@fivespoonspress.com>
Date: Sun, Jun 29 at 10:49 PM
To: Elliot Rowe <elliot@salatowest.com>

MOMA would be great, but either/or!

Subject: Re: (no subject)
From: Elliot Rowe <elliot@salatowest.com>
Date: Sun, Jun 29 at 11:30 PM
To: Madeline Whittaker <madeline@fivespoonspress.com>

Haha. K. Why don't I just text you when I get off work later and we can figure something out?

David

Yoo. Out in your hood, you around?

Jun 30, 10:32 PM

Elliot

Nah just getting home. Madeline's on her way over.

Jun 30, 10:34 PM

David

Must be nice having someone come over at 10:30 on a school night.

Jun 30, 10:36 PM

Elliot

Being in a relationship has its perks.

Jun 30, 10:42 PM

You around this week? Drinks Wednesday?

Jun 30, 10:44 PM

David

Done.

Jun 30, 10:45 PM

JULY

Madeline

Hey, sorry I missed your call last night. Was asleep . . . How was it?

Jul 8, 9:45 AM

Elliot

Super fun. Sweaty! Girl Talk shows are hilarious. Lottta shirtless dudes bro'in out hard.

Jul 8, 11:54 AM

Madeline

Yeah, I wish I could have gone. Hard to make it out to Bushwick at 11pm on a Monday . . .

Jul 8, 12:56 PM

Elliot

I hear u.

Jul 8, 2:03 PM

I'll call u later.

Jul 8, 2:34 PM

How were parent-teacher conferences? Awesome as ever?

As for me (shocker) so this is going to sound . . . well, however it sounds, but: I'm feeling a strange lack of effort on Elliot's part in the past few weeks. I'm the only one who tries to make plans these days, as opposed to what he does, which is just ask "what I'm up to," which is infuriating (what am I up to? what are you up to?). Basically, I sense an intangible demotion from girlfrIend to fuck buddy.

Except we aren't even really fucking right now.

The other night we kind of flopped into bed in a way that practically felt like we should have been putting on our PJs. We kind of touched each other but it was half-assed and soon we were both in our separate corners. We may as well have just taken a chainsaw and chopped the bed in half. And then I woke up in the AM and he was dead asleep in that way that only boys can sleep. So eventually I got up and walked to get us coffee. And it was fine . . . but also kind of not fine?

Then I don't hear from him for a day and a half and then I get this gem (I'm just going to copy and paste):

Subject: hiya!
From: Elliot Rowe <elliot@salatowest.com>
Date: Thu, Jul 10 at 11:03 AM
To: Madeline Whittaker <madeline@fivespoonspress.com>

Hey hey,

Just over at Broome Street Cafe doing a little bill paying/ housekeeping.

So I kind of have a work-related question for you: Is it crazy for someone who isn't a "name" (cough cough) to try to sell a cookbook? I was thinking there's something really cool about the concept of "Food That Chefs Cook for Other Chefs"—so like the stuff I whip up late-night when I'm trying to feed a bunch of starving Mexican line cooks using whatever's left over from the night, or when we're all at someone's apartment and it's 4 in the morning and there's just a bunch of random crap in the fridge. So, like, things that are easily executable and don't require any prep time. And since most restaurant kitchens have workers from like 15 different countries, the stuff we make for each other (stuff that never makes its way to an actual menu, mind you) usually incorporates a ton of different flavors.

Does that make any sense? I actually think it could be pretty awesome, but no idea how hard it is to get a cookbook going if you're not, like, Gwyneth Paltrow.

We still on for dinner tonight? Was thinking casual. Ramen?

Subject: Re: (no subject)
From: Emily Roberts <emilyrobertshere@gmail.com>
Date: Thu, Jul 10 at 2:30 PM
To: Madeline Whittaker <madeline@fivespoonspress.com>

Parent-teacher night was fine. The parents are always more emotional than the kids. Speaking of immature adults, you need to reduce this down to its basic parts. A white whine reduction, if you will. Get it? Because you're white and whining and work with food? I slay me. ANYWAY.

You're spinning. Basically he's taking you for granted but I don't think that necessarily means he's disinterested.

If you want my opinion (obviously): it's not the no sex that would piss me off . . . it's the total lack of acknowledgment of the weird night, the kind of nonfight, followed by the favor-asking. It's just not great that his next contact is asking you about a work thing.

Subject: Re: (no subject)
From: Madeline Whittaker <madeline@fivespoonspress.com>
Date: Thu, Jul 10 at 3:05 PM
To: Emily Roberts <emilyrobertshere@gmail.com>

Yeah, the cookbook thing is killing me. Because he's clearly giving it more thought than he's giving us. This is the longest email I've received from him in forever. I feel like a whale. You know how the Eskimos kill, like, a couple a year and then they use every single part? I am his entertainment, I got us that hotel, I give him stuff to read, I have sex with him (usually), and now—oh goodie—maybe he can use me to help his career.

When I got this, the first thing I thought was: I guess we're not using each other for sex anymore and he's moved on to a different part of the whale.

I can also feel the dam breaking . . . It takes so little for me to switch the topic of conversation to Elliot or to complain about him, and not just with you. With coworkers.

I am going to write him back on the cookbook front, pretending that he's not asking for MY help but advice in general. Because, taken at face value, that's what this email is. Fucking general.

Subject: Re: hiya!
From: Madeline Whittaker <madeline@fivespoonspress.com>
Date: Thu, Jul 10 at 5:06 PM
To: Elliot Rowe <elliot@salatowest.com>

Hey,

I think it's a solid idea. If you really think there's something to it, you should put together a proposal. All proposals look different. Basically I'd gather the meat (haha) of the book to make sure there's enough—like a list of recipes to see if this is just a trend you've noticed a few times or if there's so much information, you know you'll have to cut. And then also explore comparison titles. Look on Amazon or go to the bookstore and see what's out there and how it's doing. And you might want to play down the "using Mexican laborers for their recipes and making money off them" angle or reframe it. Up to you. Then you should probably get an agent who either specializes or has experience with cookbooks. One good way to find one is to look in the back of cookbooks you admire and read the acknowledgments page and then google the agents for contact information . . . or you can also send your proposal directly to a bunch of different publishing houses. If you're worried about not being Gwyneth Paltrow (who isn't?), you can always start a blog— develop a platform and get the attention of food editors that way. Hope that helps!

Ramen sounds good.

David

Yoo. What're you up to later? That chick from the Girl Talk show wants to hang with some friends and while I know you're spoken for, it would be nice to have you there for emotional support.

Jul 11, 7:42 PM

Elliot

Ugh, I wish. Supposed to go meet up with Mad and some of her friends after work.

Jul 11, 7:48 PM

David

Such a good boyfriend.

Jul 11, 7:52 PM

Elliot

Yeah. I'll hit you later but pretty sure I'm out of commission all night.

Jul 11, 7:58 PM

David

You sound really thrilled about it!

Jul 11, 8:02 PM

Elliot

Hmm. Actually could prob meet you for a quick drink before . . .

Jul 11, 8:06 PM

Madeline

Hopefully you've left the dungeon/
kitchen . . . you comin'?

Jul 11, 9:56 PM

Elliot

Sorry, just got in a cab. Be there in
like 15 . . .

Jul 11, 10:11 PM

Madeline

Hey . . . rumblings from people about moving
to a less crowded spot in the hood. Meet at
destination tk or I can head out if you're close . . .

Jul 11, 10:24 PM

Elliot

How long do u think you'll be there for?

Jul 11, 10:32 PM

Madeline

I don't know. I thought you were
15 minutes out either way!

Jul 11, 10:33 PM

Elliot

I was, just coming from a little further uptown.

Jul 11, 10:36 PM

Madeline

Uptown? Color me confused. If i'm not here when you arrive, text me and I'll tell u where we wound up. Will try to look at my phone . . .

Jul 11, 10:37 PM

Elliot

Totally! Yeah, sorry, I got sidetracked.

Jul 11, 10:38 PM

Elliot

Dude I think I'm starting to lose my mind with Madeline.

Jul 12, 11:01 AM

Was literally like twenty minutes late to meet her yesterday and it was like I murdered her kitten when I showed up.

Jul 12, 11:02 AM

It's like everything with her has to be planned and timed and plotted on a fucking graph.

Jul 12, 11:02 AM

David

Sorry, was in hot yoga. Honestly that shit is life-changing.

Jul 12, 12:04 PM

I didn't know Madeline got a kitten.

Jul 12, 12:05 PM

Elliot

She doesn't have a kitten. It's a metaphor.

Jul 12, 12:11 PM

David

Oh. Well. Welcome to being in a relationship. People plan shit more than a day in advance. And organize their schedules around other people's schedules. Also reservations are a thing.

Jul 12, 12:12 PM

Also, I told you to leave after one drink.

Jul 12, 12:13 PM

Elliot

I've been in a relationship before.

Jul 12, 12:14 PM

David

Yeah, with someone who was somehow flakier than you.

Jul 12, 1:05 PM

Let me ask you a question: Are you sure you even really like Madeline? Or do you just like the "idea" of her?

Jul 12, 1:06 PM

Elliot

I mean, I definitely like her.

Jul 12, 1:07 PM

David

Because the only thing that's really changed over the past few months is now it's real and it requires work.

Jul 12, 1:10 PM

Elliot

Hmm.

Jul 12, 1:15 PM

David

Lol.

Jul 12, 1:15 PM

You're like a dude who psyched himself up to climb a mountain, got to the top—then looked around and wondered why he bothered climbing a tall mountain when he could have just walked up some hills.

Jul 12, 1:17 PM

(that was a metaphor too)

Jul 12, 1:18 PM

Elliot

Yeah I got that.

Jul 12, 1:19 PM

David

So what are you going to do?

Jul 12, 1:20 PM

Elliot

I don't know. I really hate conflict.

Jul 12, 1:21 PM

David

So, what, your plan is to just slowly make the situation so untenable that you force her to break up with you?

Jul 12, 1:22 PM

Elliot

I didn't say it was a good plan.

Jul 12, 1:22 PM

Madeline

Hopefully you've left the dungeon/
kitchen . . . you comin'?

Jul 11, 9:56 PM

Elliot

Sorry, just got in a cab. Be there in
like 15 . . .

Jul 11, 10:11 PM

Madeline

Hey . . . rumblings from people about moving
to a less crowded spot in the hood. Meet at
destination tk or I can head out if you're close . . .

Jul 11, 10:24 PM

Subject: image attached
From: Madeline Whittaker <madeline@fivespoonspress.com>
Date: Sat, Jul 12 at 1:05 PM
To: Emily Roberts <emilyrobertshere@gmail.com>

Okay something is UP.

The other night, he was supposed to meet me at the Ear Inn and
he shows up *hours* late and drunk. So apparently he's "stressed at
work" but not so swamped that he couldn't have drinks with David
first when he was supposed to be meeting me. And it's not like I don't
know David—he could have brought him. I feel like that "New Yorker"
cartoon: "How about never—is never good for you?"

Subject: Re: image attached
From: Emily Roberts <emilyrobertshere@gmail.com>
Date: Sat, Jul 12 at 1:42 PM
To: Madeline Whittaker <madeline@fivespoonspress.com>

"Stressed." How fucking stressful is it to add monkfish to a menu?

Subject: Re: image attached
From: Madeline Whittaker <madeline@fivespoonspress.com>
Date: Sat, Jul 12 at 1:45 PM
To: Emily Roberts <emilyrobertshere@gmail.com>

Trying to convince myself that he is legitimately busy and confused by the logistics of planning and it's not that he's stopped trying and just kind of wants to use me when I'm around . . . It's like I'm dating the President of these United States because only the President has the actual schedule that Elliot claims to have.

Though, I'm screwed either way. Because if I'm being demoted/used, that's not good. And if he's too stupid to tell time or read a calendar? Well . . . is that a person I need to be dating?

Subject: Re: image attached
From: Emily Roberts <emilyrobertshere@gmail.com>
Date: Sat, Jul 12 at 1:53 PM
To: Madeline Whittaker <madeline@fivespoonspress.com>

I am with you, sister. I get it. I've been there. Door #1: Boy is a jerk. Door #2: Boy is not a jerk but emotionally retarded. Door #3: A pile of cats and vibrators and chocolate and one-night stands. And then it gets super confusing when more than one door is open at the same time.

But there is another possibility, you know, to Elliot's "totes cred, yo." (I am not a fan of his constant abbreviations.)

And that is the possibility that he thinks everything IS cool. And he'll work it out on his own if you let him.

I know you're afraid you're going to lose him but you're not some random psycho girl who keeps calling him after two dates. You're his girlfriend. Man up and act like it. Just call him and be like "hey . . . I need to take our temperature real quick."

x

Subject: Re: image attached
From: Madeline Whittaker <madeline@fivespoonspress.com>
Date: Sat, Jul 12 at 2:00 PM
To: Emily Roberts <emilyrobertshere@gmail.com>

No. Sorry and I love you but this is easy for you to say because you're not in this relationship.

Subject: Re: image attached
From: Emily Roberts <emilyrobertshere@gmail.com>
Date: Sat, Jul 12 at 2:02 PM
To: Madeline Whittaker <madeline@fivespoonspress.com>

Oh yes, I am.

I'm calling you (because I'm putting my money where my mouth is and you have done something that's upset me and I'd like to resolve it before I want to straight up murder your ass).

The agenda for this phone call will go as follows: a) fuck your "I love you buts . . ." b) all I do is listen to this shit while being single myself and while you rarely ask about MY love life and I hold your hand every step of the way because that's what friends do.

If you have any other agenda items to add, do let me know.

Subject: SORRY AGAIN
From: Madeline Whittaker <madeline@fivespoonspress.com>
Date: Sat, Jul 12 at 2:25 PM
To: Emily Roberts <emilyrobertshere@gmail.com>

I love you lots. I'm an asshole. As you were.

x

Subject: Re: SORRY AGAIN
From: Emily Roberts <emilyrobertshere@gmail.com>
Date: Sat, Jul 12 at 2:31 PM
To: Madeline Whittaker <madeline@fivespoonspress.com>

You are not an asshole. You're just sensitive and a wee bit crazy right now.

Love you too.

x

A FEW DAYS LATER...

Madeline

And how is our day going?

Jul 16, 12:34 PM

Elliot

Suuuper busy. You?

Jul 16, 4:15 PM

Madeline

Going well, too.

Jul 16, 7:15 PM

--------Forwarded Message-------
Subject: REMINDER: BOOK OF MORMON, EUGENE O'NEILL THEATRE
From: noreply@ticketmaster.com
To: Elliot Rowe

Elliot Rowe,

This is a reminder that your "Book of Mormon" show at the Eugene O'Neill Theatre (230 W. 49th Street, NY, NY, 10019) is coming up!

Subject: Fuck Me.
From: Elliot Rowe <elliot@salatowest.com>
Date: Fri, Jul 18 at 9:34 AM
To: David Meyer <davidmeyer@lathamlaw.com>

Jesus. Totally forgot I bought us tickets to this.

You think I should just take her and then do it? Or break up with her before and offer her the tickets?

Subject: Re: Fuck Me.
From: David Meyer <davidmeyer@lathamlaw.com>
Date: Fri, Jul 18 at 10:02 AM
To: Elliot Rowe <elliot@salatowest.com>

Great idea. "Sorry I put you through the emotional ringer for six months, go see some edgy musical comedy on me!"

Dude.

Subject: Re: Fuck Me.
From: Elliot Rowe <elliot@salatowest.com>
Date: Fri, Jul 18 at 10:13 AM
To: David Meyer <davidmeyer@lathamlaw.com>

I know, I know.

I definitely have to do this in person, right?

Subject: Re: Fuck Me.
From: David Meyer <davidmeyer@lathamlaw.com>
Date: Fri, Jul 18 at 10:14 AM
To: Elliot Rowe <elliot@salatowest.com>

Are you seriously asking me that?

Subject: Re: Fuck Me.
From: Elliot Rowe <elliot@salatowest.com>
Date: Fri, Jul 18 at 10:16 AM
To: David Meyer <davidmeyer@lathamlaw.com>

I'm just saying, I'd probably be able to explain myself better over
email . . .

Subject: Re: Fuck Me.
From: David Meyer <davidmeyer@lathamlaw.com>
Date: Fri, Jul 18 at 10:20 AM
To: Elliot Rowe <elliot@salatowest.com>

Elliot.
   Go to a quiet bar. Have exactly one drink. Be direct. Don't sleep
together afterwards.
   Pretty basic.

Subject: Re: Fuck Me.
From: Elliot Rowe <elliot@salatowest.com>
Date: Fri, Jul 18 at 10:24 AM
To: David Meyer <davidmeyer@lathamlaw.com>

Don't think you have to worry about the sleeping together part, but got it.

  You know I just realized that I've never actually dumped anyone before.

Subject: Re: Fuck Me.
From: David Meyer <davidmeyer@lathamlaw.com>
Date: Fri, Jul 18 at 10:27 AM
To: Elliot Rowe <elliot@salatowest.com>

That's not surprising. You're kind of a bitch.

Subject: Re: Fuck Me.
From: Elliot Rowe <elliot@salatowest.com>
Date: Fri, Jul 18 at 11:06 AM
To: David Meyer <davidmeyer@lathamlaw.com>

Thank you for saying "kind of."

Subject: Book of Mormon
From: Madeline Whittaker <madeline@fivespoonspress.com>
Date: Fri, Jul 18 at 1:30 PM
To: Emily Roberts <emilyrobertshere@gmail.com>

Oh, crap. He got tickets ages ago and it's coming right up.

But now the vibe is so incredibly off between us (see also: Def Com 1: Total Communication Breakdown). As recently as a month ago, it didn't seem like things could go this awry this fast. It was definitely a safe ticket-purchasing.

And now? he hasn't even MENTIONED anything and he was the one who asked. What do I do?

Subject: Re: Book of Mormon
From: Emily Roberts <emilyrobertshere@gmail.com>
Date: Fri, Jul 18 at 1:53 PM
To: Madeline Whittaker <madeline@fivespoonspress.com>

The insensitive thing to say here is "relieve your stress by giving the tickets to me" right? They are, like 400 bucks, right?

One of us is operating on a public school teacher's salary.

Maybe he's trying to get *you* to break up with him.

Subject: Re: Book of Mormon
From: Madeline Whittaker <madeline@fivespoonspress.com>
Date: Fri, Jul 18 at 2:01 PM
To: Emily Roberts <emilyrobertshere@gmail.com>

Ha! If he wants to break up with me, he'd better do it himself. I've already done all the heavy lifting in this relationship—I'm not going to dump myself, too.

ONE WEEK LATER...

David

Did you do it?

Jul 28, 9:30 PM

Elliot

Shut up.

Jul 28, 9:34 PM

David

Lol.

Jul 28, 9:41 PM

AUGUST

Subject: Hey
From: Madeline Whittaker <madeline@fivespoonspress.com>
Date: Sun, Aug 3 at 11:06 AM
To: Elliot Rowe <elliot@salatowest.com>

Hi hi,

So just looking at my trusty calendar here and it looks like "The Book of Mormon" is upon us. I have not seen a Broadway show since "Wicked" and that was with my mom. I forget how this works, but I assume you have the tickets in your possession? Should we meet up beforehand or at the theater? Lmk.

M

Subject: Re: Hey
From: Elliot Rowe <elliot@salatowest.com>
Date: Sun, Aug 3 at 11:15 AM
To: Madeline Whittaker <madeline@fivespoonspress.com>

Actually, you around tonight? Wanna grab a drink?

-------- Forwarded Message --------
Subject: Re: Hey
From: Elliot Rowe <elliot@salatowest.com>
Date: Sun, Aug 3 at 11:15 AM
To: Madeline Whittaker <madeline@fivespoonspress.com>

Actually, you around tonight? Wanna grab a drink?

Subject: Hey
From: Madeline Whittaker <madeline@fivespoonspress.com>
Date: Sun, Aug 3 at 11:06 AM
To: Elliot Rowe <elliot@salatowest.com>

Hi hi,
    So just looking at my trusty calendar here and it looks like . . .

Subject: [Fwd: Re: Hey]
From: Madeline Whittaker <madeline@fivespoonspress.com>
Date: Sun, Aug 3 at 11:19 AM
To: Emily Roberts <emilyrobertshere@gmail.com>

I am so totally getting dumped.

Subject: Re: [Fwd: Re: Hey]
From: Emily Roberts <emilyrobertshere@gmail.com>
Date: Sun, Aug 3 at 12:46 PM
To: Madeline Whittaker <madeline@fivespoonspress.com>

Oy. It's posssible he feels the same weirdness you do and just wants to see you sooner rather than later to make it go away . . . ?

Nope, nope. Dumped dumped dumpety-dumped. I'm telling you. Elliot doesn't "grab a drink." I don't think we've ever been together and not drank. I'm not saying we're alcoholics, just that . . . "grab a drink" to me is super "I'm going to get in and out and do this in public so you don't make a scene" whereas "hang out" or even "haven't seen you!" would be different. I know it sounds like a small thing but it's not . . . I know him. The "sorry for the short notice" also bothers me on a number of levels I can't even get into.

Subject: (no subject)
From: Elliot Rowe <elliot@salatowest.com>
Date: Sun, Aug 3 at 10:54 PM
To: David Meyer <davidmeyer@lathamlaw.com>

Well that did not go over well.

Subject: Re: (no subject)
From: David Meyer <davidmeyer@lathamlaw.com>
Date: Sun, Aug 3 at 10:56 PM
To: Elliot Rowe <elliot@salatowest.com>

One second getting popcorn.

Okay . . . begin.

Subject: Re: (no subject)
From: Elliot Rowe <elliot@salatowest.com>
Date: Sun, Aug 3 at 10:58 PM
To: David Meyer <davidmeyer@lathamlaw.com>

Do you want me to start with the part where she called me "an emotional vegetable" and said we should "just pull the plug," or the part where she said that I was more interested in being "in a school play about a relationship than in real intimacy"? I have a lot of starting points. Or when she accused me of using her to get a cookbook deal? (Which, sorry, but I didn't need your help to tell me to use Google.)

The ending point was that she basically told me to fuck off.

At one point, she got up to go to the bathroom, and the bartender comes over, pours me a shot of tequila, and goes, "This one's on the house, buddy." So . . . yeah.

Subject: Re: (no subject)
From: David Meyer <davidmeyer@lathamlaw.com>
Date: Sun, Aug 3 at 11:02 PM
To: Elliot Rowe <elliot@salatowest.com>

The school play metaphor is definitely better than my mountain climbing one. What did you say?

Subject: Re: (no subject)
From: Elliot Rowe <elliot@salatowest.com>
Date: Sun, Aug 3 at 11:06 PM
To: David Meyer <davidmeyer@lathamlaw.com>

Well I started off by saying that it was obvious this wasn't working and that we just fundamentally weren't (aren't) a good match. Which I thought she would respond to, but she just kind of looked at me, like, "and . . . ?" so I kept going, and said that I didn't feel like this had any long-term potential and so I didn't want to waste her time—and that was the line that really set her off. I mean I wasn't expecting her to say, "You're totally right about everything, glad we're on the same page, by the way I have a great girl for you!" And I probably did not handle this in the most efficient way, which I guess is why she really bristled at the "don't want to waste her time" line. But I still wasn't expecting this much, uh, resistance. I mean, she kept being like, "Well, if you do X, Y, and Z differently and text me back quicker and make plans and just be more 'present' things won't be this difficult." Which was basically arguing MY point of us fundamentally not being a good match, but I don't think she appreciated my connecting those dots.

Also I hate the word "present." Like I'm the only person in New York on my fucking cell phone.

Subject: Re: (no subject)
From: David Meyer <davidmeyer@lathamlaw.com>
Date: Sun, Aug 3 at 11:07 PM
To: Elliot Rowe <elliot@salatowest.com>

Wow. I'm sorry, man. That's a bummer.

I mean I genuinely do like Madeline and did think there was a universe in which it worked, but I hear where you're coming from. You can't force it if it's not working.

Well, I guess you can, if you really like someone. That's presumably how people stay married.

Subject: Re: (no subject)
From: Elliot Rowe <elliot@salatowest.com>
Date: Sun, Aug 3 at 11:12 PM
To: David Meyer <davidmeyer@lathamlaw.com>

That was kind of the subtext of what she was saying: if you liked me more, you'd be willing to put in the effort. Which I guess is true: if you're with someone and things aren't totally working, you ask yourself, "Is this a person I could maybe be with forever?" And if the answer is yes, then you try and figure it out, and if it's no, then that's that. Obviously the answer is going to be "no" a lot more than it's going to be "yes," so it seems somewhat masochistic to focus on why the answer is "no." And this is unlike her but she made an off-handed comment about her body not being good enough. I was like, "I eat doughnuts for breakfast four days a week, have you seen me without my shirt on?" And she was like, "Sorry, I don't mean to be superficial but I'd be interested in reading the statistics about how many supermodels get broken up with."

Subject: Re: (no subject)
From: David Meyer <davidmeyer@lathamlaw.com>
Date: Sun, Aug 3 at 11:16 PM
To: Elliot Rowe <elliot@salatowest.com>

Well the same five dudes seem to date every supermodel, so I'm pretty sure they get broken up with all the time. Otherwise the math wouldn't work.

Subject: Re: (no subject)
From: Elliot Rowe <elliot@salatowest.com>
Date: Sun, Aug 3 at 11:17 PM
To: David Meyer <davidmeyer@lathamlaw.com>

Maybe I should start going to therapy.

Subject: Re: (no subject)
From: David Meyer <davidmeyer@lathamlaw.com>
Date: Sun, Aug 3 at 11:17 PM
To: Elliot Rowe <elliot@salatowest.com>

I bet Ellie can recommend one.

Subject: yo
From: Emily Roberts <emilyrobertshere@gmail.com>
Date: Sun, Aug 3 at 9:00 PM
To: Madeline Whittaker <madeline@fivespoonspress.com>

What's happening? Is your phone dead or just your heart?

Subject: Re: yo
From: Madeline Whittaker <madeline@fivespoonspress.com>
Date: Sun, Aug 3 at 9:05 PM
To: Emily Roberts <emilyrobertshere@gmail.com>

We broke up.

Subject: Re: yo
From: Emily Roberts <emilyrobertshere@gmail.com>
Date: Sun, Aug 3 at 9:06 PM
To: Madeline Whittaker <madeline@fivespoonspress.com>

Oh lady. I'm sorry. Are you okay?

Subject: Re: yo
From: Madeline Whittaker <madeline@fivespoonspress.com>
Date: Sun, Aug 3 at 9:10 PM
To: Emily Roberts <emilyrobertshere@gmail.com>

I feel pretty wretched.
    And I see nothing bad about him. It's like black magic, getting dumped. All the things that made me anxious or unhappy and all the things that I genuinely did not find attractive in Elliot have vanished (much like the relationship itself) and it's like the past bunch of months never happened and I'm back to the night I met him and he's just this hot, charming, perfect guy . . . who

doesn't love me. And it's so bad, knowing the whole thing works in reverse for him. He did this and so I am magically transformed into someone much WORSE than I actually am.

He's telling himself, as I type, that I was wrong for him.

It's not fair.

Dying alone,
M

Subject: Re: yo
From: Emily Roberts <emilyrobertshere@gmail.com>
Date: Sun, Aug 3 at 9:14 PM
To: Madeline Whittaker <madeline@fivespoonspress.com>

I want to tell you something that will make you feel better but you are unhappy and your instinct will be to argue your way out of it. Like I want to tell you that you *can* do better and it really *is* him and has very little to do with you . . . but I've been you. I know your brain right now.

This is why I hate the movies. There's always a court of appeals for this crap in the movies. Our hero comes to a realization and goes running out of the Big Presentation to say how wrong he was . . . In real life, knowing yourself comes in 3-5 year increments. Basically: all romantic comedies should take 5 years instead of 2 hours.

So . . . what was his reasoning? What happened?

And where did this "drink" occur? His place?

I'm so sorry. i love you. this too shall pass . . .
xoxoxoxo

We met at Lucky Strike. I guess I'm grateful that we did this in a neutral booth of a restaurant that neither of us goes to that much. I'm sure neither of us wants our apartments tainted with sadness.

I walked in and I immediately knew. He got up from the table to kiss me, kind of leaned over it so the table was stabbing his groin. I was FINE. I really was. I was composed and got settled in. And he was sheepish and I was like, "So" and he was like, "So" and I was like, "What's going on with you?"

Men are fucking weasels. It's like, not only are you about to screw me over, but you are going to make me hold your hand and guide you.

He told me he wasn't ready for a serious relationship and things hadn't been great and that I "deserved better" and I was all fuck you for telling me what I "deserve." I know what I deserve. And he said that he "didn't want to waste my time." I feel like that's what you tell someone after a month, two tops. You don't get to think you're doing the right thing if you rob a bank and then confess 50 years later. That doesn't make you a good person. Obviously he's been feeling that he didn't want to do the basics of having a girlfriend for a really long time and was too chicken to say anything. And when I say basics, you know I mean basic. Like expecting someone to text you within 24 hours after you text them is not "demanding." Whatever.

He also thinks our "lifestyles" are "wildly opposite."

"He thinks our 'lifestyles' are 'wildly opposite'."

Oh, is he gay? KNEW IT.

Also . . . he's right about you deserving better, he's just the exact wrong person to say it.

Haha. Yeah. I just wonder what the thing is. You know, it's just a weird amount of time to date someone at our age. Like you either know you're not compatible or you date for years and get married. But Elliot and I never even fought. Which, looking back, is probably a bad sign. I was too scared to fight and he didn't care enough to fight.

He was like, "it's nothing you did" but it SHOULD be, you know? It should piss him off or he should get jealous on occasion. Some kind of pulse that indicates he's let me in, that he's counting on me to be good to him. I asked him if it was physical . . .

I hate this feeling. I also hate that the dumpee is forced to act like a 5-year-old (see also: "why why why why?" to everything he says). So not dignified.

But breakups aren't supposed to be dignified! Better to be emotional now, instead of six months from now.

Wait . . . why would it be physical?

I just wonder if that's The Thing. Like he says there's no one else (I believe him) and that he's not interested in dating other people (I don't believe him), so then what is it?

Every time you've broken up with someone, isn't there a secret thing you're not telling that person? Like "Babe, you're awesome but I secretly have to pretend I'm a prostitute to sleep with you because I'm not physically attracted to you and this is why I always have a stomach-ache." Or "Babe, you are arm candy and I could stare at you for hours, but conversation is painful and if you could not speak that would be good."

I wonder what my secret thing is.

Subject: Re: yo
From: Emily Roberts <emilyrobertshere@gmail.com>
Date: Sun, Aug 3 at 9:35 PM
To: Madeline Whittaker <madeline@fivespoonspress.com>

You are legally insane right now, I get that. I know it's tough to wrap our minds around but the mens, they are too dumb to know themselves like that. For us, we need logic. We need a reason. But I doubt there's a thing about you. I think it's simply that he's a child and practically nocturnal.

Subject: Re: yo
From: Madeline Whittaker <madeline@fivespoonspress.com>
Date: Sun, Aug 3 at 9:41 PM
To: Emily Roberts <emilyrobertshere@gmail.com>

Yeah, well. He basically said the same thing, that we had too many "bigger picture" problems. But none of it helps.

For the record: I know it's not actually anything physical. That part was one of the best parts, never had any problems in bed once we were really together.

Anyway, I feel like I have months of analyzing ahead of me . . . Right now I am going to do a shot of something and go to bed.

Subject: Re: yo
From: Emily Roberts <emilyrobertshere@gmail.com>
Date: Sun, Aug 3 at 9:47 PM
To: Madeline Whittaker <madeline@fivespoonspress.com>

Okay, let's hang out tomorrow.

You should take a pill.

Better than a hangover, which will make you feel worse. People take sleeping pills for a lot less.

Sincerely, Dr. Roberts, X.O.

David

I'm at will call. Where are you?

Aug 6, 7:24 PM

Elliot

Sorry, running laaaate. In cab.

Aug 6, 7:25 PM

David

Now I know how Madeline must have felt.

Aug 6, 7:25 PM

Too soon?

Aug 6, 7:29 PM

Elliot

Fuck, still five away.

Aug 6, 7:30 PM

David

lol

Aug 6, 7:30 PM

TWO WEEKS LATER...

Subject: updates svp
From: Emily Roberts <emilyrobertshere@gmail.com>
Date: Sat, Aug 23 at 10:19 AM
To: Madeline Whittaker <madeline@fivespoonspress.com>

How are we today? x

Subject: Re: updates svp
From: Madeline Whittaker <madeline@fivespoonspress.com>
Date: Sat, Aug 23 at 10:25 AM
To: Emily Roberts <emilyrobertshere@gmail.com>

Sometimes okay for whole minutes. Mostly.

I just want to pull my lip over my head and swallow.

Subject: Re: updates svp
From: Emily Roberts <emilyrobertshere@gmail.com>
Date: Sat, Aug 23 at 10:30 AM
To: Madeline Whittaker <madeline@fivespoonspress.com>

I'm sorry, lady. Are you sleeping okay? Want to hang out tonight?

x

Subject: Re: updates svp
From: Madeline Whittaker <madeline@fivespoonspress.com>
Date: Sat, Aug 23 at 10:38 AM
To: Emily Roberts <emilyrobertshere@gmail.com>

I had a dream that Tibetan scarf guy kidnapped me and somehow Elliot was the only one of all our friends who knew how to find me and everyone was begging him to come rescue me—because he was the only one who could do it—but he wouldn't pick up his phone or answer his door. I have the most obvious brain on the planet. No wonder I got dumped.

P.S. yes please, re: tonight. Honestly I feel like crawling into a ball and doing nothing but I know I should be human.
What is wrong with me?

Subject: Re: updates svp
From: Emily Roberts <emilyrobertshere@gmail.com>
Date: Sat, Aug 23 at 10:40 AM
To: Madeline Whittaker <madeline@fivespoonspress.com>

NOTHING. You willfully ignored some bad signs about a guy because there was so much good and you wanted to make it work. I don't know how to tell you not to take something as personal as this personally. But soon you will realize what I'm typing is true.
Don't make me pull up the emails and show you how nuts he was driving you, how anxiety-ridden he was making you. I'm not trying to downplay your heartbreak—it was real and it sucks—but I think there's an ego element to this as well . . . (see also: neck scarf Jared)
Elliot beat you to it. You were ready to kill him. You would have hit a wall eventually too, you really would have.

Subject: Re: updates svp
From: Madeline Whittaker <madeline@fivespoonspress.com>
Date: Sat, Aug 23 at 10:42 AM
To: Emily Roberts <emilyrobertshere@gmail.com>

Trying to let all that in but the only thing that offers any consolation, weirdly, this: "it was real."

xo

SEPTEMBER

Subject: (no subject)
From: David Meyer <davidmeyer@lathamlaw.com>
Date: Fri, Sep 12 at 9:42 AM
To: Elliot Rowe <elliot@salatowest.com>

I can barely type right now. How you holding up?

Subject: Re: (no subject)
From: Elliot Rowe <elliot@salatowest.com>
Date: Fri, Sep 12 at 11:11 AM
To: David Meyer <davidmeyer@lathamlaw.com>

So glad you asked.

So I was literally a block away from my house when I get a text from that girl Leslie being like, "You out?" I tell her that I'm basically back at my house—she says she's going home too, do I want to come over? Obviously. So I'm in a cab on my way to her place, when she calls me and is like, "Bring pizza, I'm hungry." I try telling her that there's no pizza place around her that's open and she's like, "Go to Rosario's, they'll definitely be open" in that drunk girl way I know I can't argue with. So I'm like *fine*, and make the cab turn around and go to Rosario's. I wait on line for like 10 minutes, get the pizza, and am about to get another cab when I get a text from her: "Bring beer too." So I go to a bodega, get a six-pack, get in a cab, and finally get to her place. Ring the door—no answer. Ring again. No answer. Call her on the phone, no answer. She just passed out. At this point, it's starting to rain, so I can't even get a cab back to my place, and I end up having to call an Uber to come get me. Surge pricing, too.

Between the cabs, pizza, beer, and transport, I spent $70 in less than forty-five minutes.

Is it crazy I kind of miss Madeline?

Don't know if I'd call it crazy, but it's definitely predictable.

ONE WEEK LATER...

Subject: Hey
From: Elliot Rowe <elliot@salatowest.com>
Date: Thu, Sep 18 at 6:02 PM
To: Madeline Whittaker <madeline@fivespoonspress.com>

Hey Madeline,

How's it going? Kind of weird having to be so formal in an email to you, but, uh, yeah.

Anyway, just wanted to let you know that I still have that cashmere cardigan of yours. I probably wouldn't have said anything if it was, like, cotton, or even a merino wool blend, but, you know, cashmere. You probably want it back.

Lemme know what's easiest for you—happy to bring it by, send it over, or leave it here for you to pick up.

Hope you're well. I saw one of your authors profiled in Sunday Styles last week and felt a twinge of pride. Glad work is going good.

—e

-------- Forwarded Message --------
Subject: Hey
From: Elliot Rowe <elliot@salatowest.com>
Date: Thu, Sep 18 at 6:02 PM
To: Madeline Whittaker <madeline@fivespoonspress.com>

Hey Madeline,
    How's it going? Kind of weird having to be so formal in an email . . .

Subject: [Fwd: Hey]
From: Madeline Whittaker <madeline@fivespoonspress.com>
Date: Thu, Sep 18 at 6:06 PM
To: Emily Roberts <emilyrobertshere@gmail.com>

So 1.5 million years later . . . this arrives.

Subject: Re: [Fwd: Hey]
From: Emily Roberts <emilyrobertshere@gmail.com>
Date: Thu, Sep 18 at 7:01 PM
To: Madeline Whittaker <madeline@fivespoonspress.com>

**Jesus. Not really a fan of the uber-chummy tone there. I mean . . .
how are you feeling? And do you need me to get the sweater?**

From: Madeline Whittaker <madeline@fivespoonspress.com>
Date: Thu, Sep 18 at 7:03 PM
To: Emily Roberts <emilyrobertshere@gmail.com>

I feel like he is, uh, right. It is, uh, weird to be so ugh formal and so soon.

Look: I don't think he strung me along cruelly. I don't think he is a sociopath.

But no, you do not get to be a gentleman by saying "whatever's easiest for you." I know him. I know what he's trying to do. And no, you do not get to participate in my success or feel "proud" of me because you see something you know I had a part in in the Sunday fucking Styles section.

THAT is insensitive. Like I'm already becoming this kind of a thing he dated. The Cookbook Chick.

And work is going "well," not "good." The alternative doesn't make you easy/breezy, it makes you retarded.

Subject: Re: [Fwd: Hey]
From: Emily Roberts <emilyrobertshere@gmail.com>
Date: Thu, Sep 18 at 7:05 PM
To: Madeline Whittaker <madeline@fivespoonspress.com>

Right. So do you want me to get the sweater?

Subject: Re: Hey
From: Madeline Whittaker <madeline@fivespoonspress.com>
Date: Sun, Sep 21 at 8:02 PM
To: Elliot Rowe <elliot@salatowest.com>

Hi Elliot,

I'll give Emily your contact info so you guys can arrange a time for her to get the sweater, as she will be in your neighborhood later this week.

—Madeline

Subject: Re: Hey
From: Elliot Rowe <elliot@salatowest.com>
Date: Sun, Sep 21 at 9:04 PM
To: Madeline Whittaker <madeline@fivespoonspress.com>

That works.

Also, do you by chance happen to have my Mets hat? It's not at the restaurant and I can't find it here, so I'm hoping it's at your place. If you have it, would be great if you could give it to Emily as well.

—Elliot

Subject: Re: Hey
From: Madeline Whittaker <madeline@fivespoonspress.com>
Date: Sun, Sep 21 at 9:09 PM
To: Elliot Rowe <elliot@salatowest.com>

No, I don't have it. Though you haven't been at my place since before my cleaning lady was here weeks ago and it's possible she tossed it.

Subject: Re: Hey
From: Elliot Rowe <elliot@salatowest.com>
Date: Sun, Sep 21 at 9:15 PM
To: Madeline Whittaker <madeline@fivespoonspress.com>

Well, I don't think she'd throw it away—but no worries. They are replaceable.

Subject: Re: Hey
From: Madeline Whittaker <madeline@fivespoonspress.com>
Date: Sun, Sep 21 at 10:02 PM
To: Elliot Rowe <elliot@salatowest.com>

Cool. Glad you can go out and get a new one.

-------- Forwarded Message --------
Subject: Re: Hey
From: Madeline Whittaker <madeline@fivespoonspress.com>
Date: Sun, Sep 21 at 9:09 PM
To: Elliot Rowe <elliot@salatowest.com>

No, I don't have it. Though you haven't been at my place since . . .

Subject: Re: Hey
From: Elliot Rowe <elliot@salatowest.com>
Date Sun, Sep 21 at 9:04 PM
To: Madeline Whittaker <madeline@fivespoonspress.com>

That works.
 Also, do you by chance happen to have my Mets hat? It's not . . .

Subject: Re: Hey
From: Madeline Whittaker <madeline@fivespoonspress.com>
Date: Sun, Sep 21 at 8:02 PM
To: Elliot Rowe <elliot@salatowest.com>

Hi Elliot,
 I'll give Emily your contact info so you guys can arrange . . .

Subject: [Fwd: Re: Hey]
From: Madeline Whittaker <madeline@fivespoonspress.com>
Date: Sun, Sep 21 at 9:20 PM
To: Emily Roberts <emilyrobertshere@gmail.com>

Guess what I don't have? A cleaning lady.

Guess what I *do* have . . .

Subject: Re: [Fwd: Re: Hey]
From: Emily Roberts <emilyrobertshere@gmail.com>
Date: Sun, Sep 21 at 9:23 PM
To: Madeline Whittaker <madeline@fivespoonspress.com>

WHOA. what will become of the hat?

Subject: Re: [Fwd: Re: Hey]
From: Madeline Whittaker <madeline@fivespoonspress.com>
Date: Sun, Sep 21 at 9:24 PM
To: Emily Roberts <emilyrobertshere@gmail.com>

To be shoved down the garbage chute when I see fit.

Subject: Re: [Fwd: Re: Hey]
From: Emily Roberts <emilyrobertshere@gmail.com>
Date: Sun, Sep 21 at 9:26 PM
To: Madeline Whittaker <madeline@fivespoonspress.com>

You have an actual garbage chute? That's so cool.

-------Forwarded Message------
Subject: Re: Hey
From: Madeline Whittaker <madeline@fivespoonspress.com>
Date: Sun, Sep 21 at 10:02 PM
To: Elliot Rowe <elliot@salatowest.com>

Cool. Glad you can go out and get a new one.

Subject: Re: Hey
From: Elliot Rowe <elliot@salatowest.com>
Date: Sun, Sep 21 at 9:15 PM
To: Madeline Whittaker <madeline@fivespoonspress.com>

Well, I don't think she'd throw it away—but no worries. They are replaceable.

Subject: [Fwd: Re: Hey]
From: Elliot Rowe <elliot@salatowest.com>
Date: Sun, Sep 21 at 10:05 PM
To: David Meyer <davidmeyer@lathamlaw.com>

So do you think she still likes me?

Subject: Re: [Fwd: Re: Hey]
From: David Meyer <davidmeyer@lathamlaw.com>
Date: Sun, Sep 21 at 10:11 PM
To: Elliot Rowe <elliot@salatowest.com>

Holy shit.
    That's not even passive-aggressive. It's aggressive-aggressive.
    Wow.
    I would say no, she does not still like you.

Subject: Re: [Fwd: Re: Hey]
From: Elliot Rowe <elliot@salatowest.com>
Date: Sun, Sep 21 at 10:14 PM
To: David Meyer <davidmeyer@lathamlaw.com>

I'm tempted to just write back "Found it!" to see how she responds.

Subject: Re: [Fwd: Re: Hey]
From: David Meyer <davidmeyer@lathamlaw.com>
Date: Sun, Sep 21 at 10:15 PM
To: Elliot Rowe <elliot@salatowest.com>

I think just take the high road.

That was a great hat though. Sorry pal.

-------- Forwarded Message --------
Subject: [Fwd: Madeline's Sweater]
From: Emily Roberts <emilyrobertshere@gmail.com>
Date: Mon, Sep 22 at 8:20 PM
To: Madeline Whittaker <madeline@fivespoonspress.com>

Fyi. It's all happening.

Subject: Madeline's Sweater
From: Emily Roberts <emilyrobertshere@gmail.com>
Date: Mon, Sep 22 at 11:15 AM
To: Elliot Rowe <elliot@salatowest.com>

Hey Elliot—

I am going to be in your neck of the woods after work on Thursday and Friday. Will you text me your address/times that work for you and I can grab M's sweater from you? I'm free after 6:30 both days.

Thanks.

Emily
917-207-4125

Subject: Re: Madeline's Sweater
From: Elliot Rowe <elliot@salatowest.com>
Date: Mon, Sep 22 at 12:32 PM
To: Emily Roberts <emilyrobertshere@gmail.com>

Hey Emily,
   How about Thursday evening? You've been to my place. It's 157 Ludlow Street in case you don't remember.

—Elliot

Subject: Re: Madeline's Sweater
From: Emily Roberts <emilyrobertshere@gmail.com>
Date: Mon, Sep 22 at 12:45 PM
To: Elliot Rowe <elliot@salatowest.com>

Evening is kinda vague. Is there a specific time?

Also, apt. #? Cell #?

Subject: Re: Madeline's Sweater
From: Elliot Rowe <elliot@salatowest.com>
Date: Mon, Sep 22 at 3:06 PM
To: Emily Roberts <emilyrobertshere@gmail.com>

How about 6:30? And it's apt.2B. The buzzer only occasionally works but the door is usually open.

Subject: Re: [Fwd: Madeline's Sweater]
From: Madeline Whittaker <madeline@fivespoonspress.com>
Date: Mon, Sep 22 at 8:25 PM
To: Emily Roberts <emilyrobertshere@gmail.com>

Thanks for the update.
    This kind of made me laugh, which is a good thing. You see what I dealt with? I am now realizing that it's not that I am so anal but that any woman who manages to pass through the Elliot "too cool for school" gauntlet will have to deal with this.
    I frequently got texts from him that were like "meet here later?" and then I got to be in the delightful position of "where are you? Where is here?" and "9:30?"

OCTOBER

Subject: unsocial media
From: Madeline Whittaker <madeline@fivespoonspress.com>
Date: Thu, Oct 2 at 11:15 AM
To: Emily Roberts <emilyrobertshere@gmail.com>

So I unfollowed him on Twitter. I mean, the idea of following him or not is irrelevant. I'm still going to spot-check the hell out of that account and see if he's following new girls. Which is actually a lot more efficient than Instagram where I have to check every half hour to see whose photos he's liked.

Subject: Re: unsocial media
From: Emily Roberts <emilyrobertshere@gmail.com>
Date: Thu, Oct 2 at 11:45 AM
To: Madeline Whittaker <madeline@fivespoonspress.com>

Good for you, lady! But don't even spot-check.
    I thought he didn't even tweet that much anyway. You could always just keep following him because, you know: who cares.

Subject: Re: unsocial media
From: Madeline Whittaker <madeline@fivespoonspress.com>
Date: Thu, Oct 2 at 11:48 AM
To: Emily Roberts <emilyrobertshere@gmail.com>

Well . . . now I can't! Already unfollowed and he has just enough followers that he won't notice (unless he's spot-checking me too . . . wishful thinking but kinda doubtful?) and just enough that he definitely *will* notice if I refollow him like a psycho.

Subject: Re: unsocial media
From: Emily Roberts <emilyrobertshere@gmail.com>
Date: Thu, Oct 2 at 12:00 PM
To: Madeline Whittaker <madeline@fivespoonspress.com>

Well, at least you're not overthinking it.

Subject: Re: unsocial media
From: Madeline Whittaker <madeline@fivespoonspress.com>
Date: Thu, Oct 2 at 12:08 PM
To: Emily Roberts <emilyrobertshere@gmail.com>

That reminds me. I found the perfect gift for you:
http://phototrove.com/wp-content/kid-screaming-with-middle-finger.jpg

---

Subject: Re: unsocial media
From: Emily Roberts <emilyrobertshere@gmail.com>
Date: Thu, Oct 2 at 12:20 PM
To: Madeline Whittaker <madeline@fivespoonspress.com>

Awwww. There she is. I've missed you, Madeline. x

ONE WEEK LATER...

Subject: don't kill me
From: Madeline Whittaker <madeline@fivespoonspress.com>
Date: Wed, Oct 8 at 1:30 PM
To: Emily Roberts <emilyrobertshere@gmail.com>

Confession: I have backslided and looked through every day this week. And you're right, he hasn't produced a single thought beyond retweeting Louis C.K. So in my better moments I think, "He's too heartbroken to tweet!" and in my worse I think, "He's having too much sex with random skanks to tweet!" And all of these moments are, naturally, underpinned by the realization that I am going to be alone forever and never have kids but maybe that's good because all boys turn into assholes and all girls turn into humans who react to men being assholes.

The good news? Breakup weight loss = awesome Instagram fodder.

I'm having drinks with a hot new dude from work tonight. A "welcome to the office" thing. It will be nice to be around a human with a penis who doesn't want to run from me.

Aggg! Slow the depression roll. listen to your brain, it's smarter than your heart right now.

You know, they're all assholes until one isn't. I'm sorry to say that both our asshole quotas have been, I think, unreasonably high. I think it should have ended at 26. I'm not saying I wanted to be taken off the market at 26 because um, no thank you. But I just think that 26 has a nice end-of-bs-from-guys-who-don't-know-what-they-want vibe. Like you can rent a car at 25 and then the next milestone should be "yay! 26! you're free from games!!"

But we're never free! Never! mwahahaha. Have fun with your coworker dude tonight. Are you his superior?

X

Subject: (no subject)
From: Elliot Rowe <elliot@salatowest.com>
Date: Wed, Oct 8 at 9:54 PM
To: David Meyer <davidmeyer@lathamlaw.com>

Just saw Madeline on a date.

Subject: Re: (no subject)
From: David Meyer <davidmeyer@lathamlaw.com>
Date: Wed, Oct 8 at 10:15 PM
To: Elliot Rowe <elliot@salatowest.com>

Ha. Where?

Subject: Re: (no subject)
From: Elliot Rowe <elliot@salatowest.com>
Date: Wed, Oct 8 at 10:17 PM
To: David Meyer <davidmeyer@lathamlaw.com>

It was so weird. I was in Midtown walking to the subway and wanted to catch the last two min of the Knicks game so I pop into this random pub. I'm at the bar watching the TV and out of the corner of my eye I see this couple making out. Like aggressively. And I look closer and it's MADELINE. We make eye contact for a split second, but it's not like she's gonna stop what she's doing to say something and I sure as hell wasn't gonna interrupt them. I was about to turn around, but then I didn't want it to seem like I was leaving because of her, so I just walk into the back room, where I spent the next 45 min drinking by myself waiting for them to leave.

Oh, and the Knicks lost, obviously. Pretty great.

Subject: Re: (no subject)
From: David Meyer <davidmeyer@lathamlaw.com>
Date: Wed, Oct 8 at 10:24 PM
To: Elliot Rowe <elliot@salatowest.com>

That's hilarious.
   Looking at her Instagram right now, was the dude you saw @TheRealBrian? She just started following him.
   Handsome guy. Lotta CrossFit pics. He could definitely beat you up.

Subject: Re: (no subject)
From: Elliot Rowe <elliot@salatowest.com>
Date: Wed, Oct 8 at 10:26 PM
To: David Meyer <davidmeyer@lathamlaw.com>

Been avoiding her Instagram, but yes that's him.

What's your FB password?

Subject: Re: (no subject)
From: David Meyer <davidmeyer@lathamlaw.com>
Date: Wed, Oct 8 at 10:28 PM
To: Elliot Rowe <elliot@salatowest.com>

Hotdog1212, why?

Subject: Re: (no subject)
From: Elliot Rowe <elliot@salatowest.com>
Date: Wed, Oct 8 at 10:29 PM
To: David Meyer <davidmeyer@lathamlaw.com>

Madeline unfriended me. Can only see her profile through yours.

Subject: Re: (no subject)
From: David Meyer <davidmeyer@lathamlaw.com>
Date: Wed, Oct 8 at 10:29 PM
To: Elliot Rowe <elliot@salatowest.com>

Down the rabbit hole we go.

Subject: Re: (no subject)
From: Elliot Rowe <elliot@salatowest.com>
Date: Wed, Oct 8 at 10:33 PM
To: David Meyer <davidmeyer@lathamlaw.com>

Wait, Madeline RSVP'd to Lyle's party. How does she know Lyle??

Subject: Re: (no subject)
From: David Meyer <davidmeyer@lathamlaw.com>
Date: Wed, Oct 8 at 10:36 PM
To: Elliot Rowe <elliot@salatowest.com>

It's actually Lyle's girlfriend's party. She's in publishing. They're probably work friends.

Subject: Re: (no subject)
From: Elliot Rowe <elliot@salatowest.com>
Date: Wed, Oct 8 at 10:37 PM
To: David Meyer <davidmeyer@lathamlaw.com>

Well she RSVP'd +1! I can't go now.

Subject: Re: (no subject)
From: David Meyer <davidmeyer@lathamlaw.com>
Date: Wed, Oct 8 at 10:42 PM
To: Elliot Rowe <elliot@salatowest.com>

So what, you're just going to refrain from showing up anywhere she might conceivably be for the next six months?

Subject: Re: (no subject)
From: Elliot Rowe <elliot@salatowest.com>
Date: Wed, Oct 8 at 10:44 PM
To: David Meyer <davidmeyer@lathamlaw.com>

At the bare minimum.

Subject: Re: (no subject)
From: David Meyer <davidmeyer@lathamlaw.com>
Date: Wed, Oct 8 at 10:49 PM
To: Elliot Rowe <elliot@salatowest.com>

Well, I'm still going, but good luck with that.

Subject: Re: don't kill me
From: Emily Roberts <emilyrobertshere@gmail.com>
Date: Thu, Oct 9 at 8:30 AM
To: Madeline Whittaker <madeline@fivespoonspress.com>

Just saw your missed call.

What the hell happened last night?

Subject: Re: don't kill me
From: Madeline Whittaker <madeline@fivespoonspress.com>
Date: Thu, Oct 9 at 9:02 AM
To: Emily Roberts <emilyrobertshere@gmail.com>

Haha. It was magnificent. So Brian, who yes, is superhot, and I are having a nice time, drinking bad beer and eating salmonella-laced bar food and we get a little drunk and start talking about our romantic histories and it turns out we've both just gotten out of relationships.

I will now, in the light of day, sheepishly cop to the fact that when Brian said he used to live with his girlfriend, I made it sound like Elliot and I were serious enough to live together too.

Anyway, Brian has amazing dirty-blond hair, electric-blue eyes, actual chin dimple.

Long story longer: we're griping about our exes and gathering our things to leave and we just get along so well (I'm psyched he'll be in the office) that we start joking about how much easier it would be on both of us if we could date, if we didn't work together.

Then he really dramatically kisses me and says, "Well, just this once." And we both laugh. This is the EXACT moment Elliot sashays through the door, hands in pockets of leather jacket (does one just elbow open all doors when one's fists are constantly jammed into one's pockets?) And I'm laughing for the first time in forever because for the first time in forever I'm genuinely happy and not thinking about Elliot. But then we lock eyes . . .

And I gave what was probably a too-cheerful hello (I get nervous, I turn into a fucking cheerleader). Elliot did not look happy. Just surprised. It all happened really quickly. Then we left. Not sure if Elliot saw. Crazy.

M x

P.S. I am sorry if my frequency is stuck on Elliot. Your turn to find someone as great as you (if we can dig up someone that cool).

Subject: Re: don't kill me
From: Emily Roberts <emilyrobertshere@gmail.com>
Date: Thu, Oct 9 at 9:30 AM
To: Madeline Whittaker <madeline@fivespoonspress.com>

Holy shit. I love this. I mean . . . it's all stranger than fiction, isn't it? The run-in alone would be a weird coincidence. The kiss with a hot guy? That's divine justice, sweetheart.

But yes, thank you for your P.S. It's okay. This is what friends are for . . . I am deeply invested in your well-being. Yes, also invested in mine. If we can find me a gainfully employed person who has just a little bit of a sense of humor (why are men so unfunny?), that would be swell. Also someone who doesn't mind me using "swell."

x

PS: Are you going to Lucy Cook's thing? Meet for a drink beforehand?

Subject: Tonight
From: Madeline Whittaker <madeline@fivespoonspress.com>
Date: Thu, Oct 9 at 10:41 PM
To: Emily Roberts <emilyrobertshere@gmail.com>

You're going to think I'm an insane person (too late) but last night's/ this morning's empowering fairy dust of Elliot witnessing that kiss has worn off. Lucy just started dating Lyle I-forget-his-last-name-but-he-has-dreads, a sous chef at a restaurant owned by the same guys who own Elliot's place.

Anyway, the chances of Elliot being there are good and now I kind of don't want to go.

Subject: Re: Tonight
From: Emily Roberts <emilyrobertshere@gmail.com>
Date: Thu, Oct 9 at 10:48 PM
To: Madeline Whittaker <madeline@fivespoonspress.com>

You can't let this breakup dictate where you go and don't go. That's the height of crazy. Also: I'm bored, barely know Lucy, only know her through you and I do not want to go to a party in someone's house where I know zero people. Buddy system or bust.

Subject: Re: Tonight
From: Madeline Whittaker <madeline@fivespoonspress.com>
Date: Thu, Oct 9 at 10:56 PM
To: Emily Roberts <emilyrobertshere@gmail.com>

It's not a major sacrifice. I'm not missing the Oscars . . . Hell, I'm not even missing the James Beard Awards because of Elliott. I just . . . for the same reason you don't want to go alone, I don't want to go period: just not strong enough mentally right now to be trapped in a confined space with Elliot.

Subject: Re: Tonight
From: Emily Roberts <emilyrobertshere@gmail.com>
Date: Thu, Oct 9 at 11:15 PM
To: Madeline Whittaker <madeline@fivespoonspress.com>

Fine, nutball. I shall go without you and have the best night ever!

THE NEXT DAY...

Subject: Ummmmmm . . .
From: David Meyer <davidmeyer@lathamlaw.com>
Date: Fri, Oct 10 at 12:06 PM
To: Emily Roberts <emilyrobertshere@gmail.com>

Hey Emily,

Was really nice seeing you last night (without Mom and Dad or duck). Before I give this too much thought, I'm just going to go ahead and ask: do you want to get a drink next week? Maybe Thursday? Totally understand if you feel kind of weird about this. I feel kind of weird too, which is another way of saying I didn't tell Elliot I'm doing this. But I feel like we've more than fulfilled our "friend duties" to them the past few months, so why should we let them get in the way of our eternal happiness?!

Perhaps I'm getting a little ahead of myself. But serious about the drink.

—D

Subject: Re: Ummmmmm . . .
From: Emily Roberts <emilyrobertshere@gmail.com>
Date: Fri, Oct 10 at 1:14 PM
To: David Meyer <davidmeyer@lathamlaw.com>

David,

It was great running into you. Totally ignoring the "do I mention this to Maddy" question because, well, it's a big question and one that doesn't need to be answered right now . . . unlike yours, which *does* require an answer: Thursday sounds awesome. Super fun night redux!

—E

Subject: Re: Ummmmmm . . .
From: David Meyer <davidmeyer@lathamlaw.com>
Date: Fri, Oct 10 at 1:48 PM
To: Emily Roberts <emilyrobertshere@gmail.com>

This is either a really good or a really horrendous decision. But I'm okay with that if you are.

I'll be out of the office by 7:30. Does 8:15 work for you? That should give me enough time to go home, take off my suit, deliberate on which flannel shirt to wear, and come meet you . . .

Subject: Re: Ummmmmm . . .
From: Emily Roberts <emilyrobertshere@gmail.com>
Date: Fri, Oct 10 at 2:06 PM
To: David Meyer <davidmeyer@lathamlaw.com>

Perfect.

You would think that dealing with the fallout of our two beloved pals would have made me lose all faith in relationships. Luckily, I'm a sucker for a good flannel shirt. Since you picked the easy part, you rat, I'll do the hard part: Da Silvano?

—E

Subject: Re: Ummmmmm . . .
From: David Meyer <davidmeyer@lathamlaw.com>
Date: Fri, Oct 10 at 3:12 PM
To: Emily Roberts <emilyrobertshere@gmail.com>

Mmmmm rigatoni. I like where your head is at.

You know what? I'm just going to come right out and say it. I'm over this small plate stuff. (Sorry Elliot.) Why does every trendy restaurant advertise that like it's a selling point?

Here's a novel concept: big plates. So I will actually be full when I leave. You're welcome, America.

Really looking forward to seeing you again.

Subject: (no subject)
From: Emily Roberts <emilyrobertshere@gmail.com>
Date: Fri, Oct 17 at 8:42 AM
To: David Meyer <davidmeyer@lathamlaw.com>

Good morning!

You know what's even worse than being hungover? Being hungover and having to teach long division to a bunch of kids with ADHD.

Anyway, since I just spent months doing the emotional equivalent of unfurling motivational speaking posters for my best friend, saying things like "Be yourself!" and "Don't worry about his reaction so much!" I guess it's only fair that I take my own advice and say, simply . . .

That was so awesome.

Can we do it again, like, yesterday?

NOVEMBER

Subject: So . . .
From: David Meyer <davidmeyer@lathamlaw.com>
Date: Tue, Nov 4 at 4:34 PM
To: Emily Roberts <emilyrobertshere@gmail.com>

So Elliot keeps asking me what I want to do for my birthday. Still haven't told him that I won't be in town . . .
 I'm sitting at my desk holding a quarter. Heads, I tell Elliot first. Tails, you tell Madeline first.
 Call it?

Subject: Re: So . . .
From: Emily Roberts <emilyrobertshere@gmail.com>
Date: Tue, Nov 4 at 5:15 PM
To: David Meyer <davidmeyer@lathamlaw.com>

TAILS.

(I kind of love how we're doing this btw: a little bit of chance, a little bit of trust . . .)

Subject: Re: So . . .
From: David Meyer <davidmeyer@lathamlaw.com>
Date: Tue, Nov 4 at 5:23 PM
To: Emily Roberts <emilyrobertshere@gmail.com>

I love it too. Especially that the "this" you speak of could refer to either the coin toss or two people in a . . . relationship? :) Either way, let's do this thing.

Subject: Re: So . . .
From: David Meyer <davidmeyer@lathamlaw.com>
Date: Tue, Nov 4 at 5:24 PM
To: Emily Roberts <emilyrobertshere@gmail.com>

Okay the coin bounced off the table. Shit.

I guess this means we just tell them at the same time?

Subject: Re: So . . .
From: Emily Roberts <emilyrobertshere@gmail.com>
Date: Tue, Nov 4 at 5:28 PM
To: David Meyer <davidmeyer@lathamlaw.com>

Swell.
  We can do it together via conference call this weekend from Montauk.
  Honestly, I don't know how much Madeline will even flip out. Especially since she has a nice little cushion now. She's started dating someone. He's got a job that takes place during the day, doesn't own a single piece of vinyl, and works in finance. But I like him. He raises money for hospitals or something. They have spent literally every night together this week. I haven't seen her this happy in, well, months.

Subject: Re: So . . .
From: David Meyer <davidmeyer@lathamlaw.com>
Date: Tue, Nov 4 at 5:34 PM
To: Emily Roberts <emilyrobertshere@gmail.com>

Well, Elliot's spent every night this week bitching about his various Tinder dates, so it appears order has been restored.
  Why do I have the feeling Madeline and Mr. Raises Money for Hospitals are going to get married?

I think they might! I know that's silly because it's early but this relationship is clearly easy for both of them.

They both want it and she is a very happy camper. But you want to know the A #1 reason I think it's going to work out?

She hasn't forwarded me a single email of his.

About the Authors

Neel Shah is a screenwriter in Los Angeles. He used to be a reporter at the *New York Post* and his work has appeared in *Glamour*, *GQ*, and *New York* magazine.

Skye Chatham is a writer living in New York. Her work has appeared in various publications, including *GQ* and *Maxim*.